Ursula's Prism

by

Anna Block

Gihon River Press
East Stroudsburg, PA
2011

Published by Gihon River Press

P.O. Box 88

East Stroudsburg PA. 18301

www.gihonriverpress.com

Cover Design by John Illo
Interior Drawings by Rich Sigberman

This is a work of fiction based on a true story and all
people – living or dead – events, dates and situations
are made to the best recollection of the author.
The publisher assumes no responsibility for the accuracy..

First Edition

10 9 8 7 6 5 4 3 2 1

ISBN: 978-0-981990-2-0

Library of Congress Cataloging-in-Publication Data pending

Acknowledgments

Much gratitude must be expressed to Stephen Feuer of Gihon River Press; of his unwavering belief in the project, his vision, and his ability to delegate. Without your help this story may have been lost. Thank you to Phil Sieradski for his editing and research expertise. And thank you to Maureen MacNeil, Education Director of the Anne Frank Center of New York. I am honored for the addition of your Introduction. I thank all of you for your hard work.

On a more personal note, I wish to thank Sue Tanon, my confidante, the one who spurred me on from the inception of my work. And thank you to Kathy Witmer for being a spiritual guidance and true friend. Thank you both for your immeasurable encouragement and support.

Not enough gratitude can be expressed to my mother. As a child I watched her laugh and dance, never realizing the underlying agony. It was her willingness to share these deeply traumatic moments of her childhood that allowed me to have an even deeper respect for my family and my faith. Her hopes align with mine-that in the telling of these events, maybe we can prevent these atrocities from repeating. Thank you, Mother; I am humbled yet proud to be Ursula's daughter.

God bless.

Introduction

Stories of children suffering during the Holocaust are difficult to read, yet they often inspire the human spirit to take action. Survivors' stories teach us that if society fails, we are all responsible: We must become helpers and resisters so history does not repeat itself. *Ursula's Prism*, based on a true story imaginatively retold by Ursula's daughter, Anna Block, is one such story.

It begins with the bustling Swartz family and their nanny at breakfast in Glashütte, just outside Dresden, Germany. Among the happy tumult of five children preparing for their day, Ursula's mother tells her about the life-long lessons of her special necklace with its crystal prisms: show kindness; think positive thoughts; be strong; and keep an open mind. Soon after, as armed SS soldiers arrest the family, Ursula manages to slip her mother's necklace into her pocket.

Unexpected helpers and their desire to act against the brutal Nazis appear in the story like the beautiful reflections of the seemingly magical prism. Ursula, her 12 year-old brother Ludwig, along with four other children, manage to escape from Bergen-Belsen and brave the unknown, the bitter winter countryside and starvation. Yet the power of the children's imagination and their will to live shines on every page.

Like Anne Frank's diary, the lessons in *Ursula's Prism* are many. The children learn that they cannot rely on stereotypes of soldiers and farmers to keep them safe, but must judge each person individually. They find ways to nurture themselves and keep hopeful that circumstances will improve. Ultimately, it is their loyalty to each other, their ability to ask questions, think critically and use their emotional intelligence that enables them to stay alive in the woods day after day.

With this in mind, perhaps the secrets of the necklace that Ursula shares with the other children gives them the resiliency they need to survive. It is my hope that readers of this book will find that they too possess what it takes to resist hate in today's world, and that they will pass this story along.

Maureen McNeil
Director of Education
The Anne Frank Center USA

A Note from Ursula's Daughter

For the honor of the Jewish people and nation I offer this tribute: A labor of love dedicated to the victims and survivors of the Holocaust. I submit this reverential work because even after all these years, for the survivors the torment is never over; dreams are haunted by recollections, an innocent gesture or phrase can rekindle a tormenting memory.

Within the pages of this book are my mother's memories and one must take into account her age at the time of her and her family's capture. Her childish perception of the tumult that surrounded her may have distorted some factual details, but, can one ever truly comprehend the depths of hatred and fear that plague those who suffered demoralizing atrocities at the hands of another?

Yet, amidst the dreadful, horrifying acts that exemplified the Hitler regime, an opposing power stirred. This power is the emotion that overcomes us when we witness cruelty, the emotion that forces our hearts to cry out for cessation of that inhuman transgression. This power is compassion, a force that moved many — despite great, personal danger — to help the Jews and other victims of Nazi terror to survive.

Compassion dwells within each of us, a gift from our Creator. When we use this power, we lift ourselves to a higher standard—and those we touch. Though socioeconomic conditions or mindsets of ignorance may seek to destroy our compassion for the less fortunate or for those who are different from us, we must still be able to recognize our God-given humanity and overcome this negativity. How? We can start by teaching our children the "crystal prism principles."

The "crystal prism principles," as introduced in *Ursula's Prism*, teach us respect for ourselves and others. Sharing, displaying kindness, having an open mind, having a positive attitude and keeping our word are just the basic moral elements that every human being needs instilled within them. These "principles" are not new but rather buried in our wounded souls, craving to be set free. If all would practice "the principles," a better life would be possible.

This generation and the ones to follow cannot afford to lose their compassion. We must teach it to our children and demonstrate its positive and beneficial qualities. It starts with one—one open heart, one open mind—and then, in a domino effect, all manner of negativity can be squelched.

Can we begin today?

Table of Contents

Scale: .5"=@100 miles
X - where the mechanic dropped the children off
Y - where the five children were found by the British
Z - displaced persons camp in Essen
•••••• the children's journey on foot
|||||||||| train to Bergen-Belsen

Chapter One

Ursula awakened as the morning sunlight tickled her eyelids. She teased the sun's rays, opening one eye ever so slightly. Catching a glimpse of her favorite doll, she sat up in bed and giggled with glee as she reached for it. How could she not love her brand-new doll? Poppa had just made it for her sixth birthday.

"See, pumpkin, I made it to look just like you," Poppa said. How truly he had spoken. The heart-shaped porcelain face had rosy cheeks. The head was crowned with a soft pile of strawberry blonde hair that fell in gentle waves to its shoulders. And the eyes were of such a dark blue that they seemed to be black. And now as Ursula looked into the doll's eyes she was sure she could see her parents' love beaming back at her.

Her parents, Anna and Frederick Swartz, had owned and operated a small toy factory in Dresden, Germany. The factory's reputation for finely crafted toys had been handed down for generations. And so they ran a lucrative business that enabled them to have a big house for their family (with separate living quarters for the nanny), in a little town named Glashütte, on the outskirts of Dresden. Anna worked as the company's bookkeeper and salesperson, while Frederick designed and built the toys and regulated the work of their ten employees. The business had been doing well until the Nazi army urged German citizens to boycott Jewish businesses. Then business took another grevious turn when Frederick and Anna were forced to sign the title of the factory over to the German government. Downtrodden by the criminal siege of their family legacy, but painfully aware of their need for employment, they continued their daily work in the factory.

Many times when Anna and Frederick would arrive at their factory they would find vandals had scrawled graffito on the premises, rotten vegetables smashed against the door, and a few times even worse—feces smeared on the steps. Adding to this intimidation, SS soldiers would creep by in their military vehicles and peer inside the windows.

"Go on, leave us alone," Frederick mumbled one day as the military trucks passed by the factory. He turned his head to see his wife standing near him. "I guess it's not enough that we hand our factory over to them. We wear these armbands; we paint the Star of David on our door." He raised his fist and yelled after they had passed. "You don't need to watch us so closely!"

"It is getting harder to hide things," Anna said, clutching her husband's arm. Nazi officers often made unexpected visits to scour the pages of the factory's accounts. "I heard a rumor that the SS has questioned the employees."

2

"Do you know what was said?" he asked.

"No one will admit to anything. But I see it in their eyes," Anna said as she turned to face him, "they're all scared. They've probably threatened all of them. Freddie, I'm scared too."

"We've been sending money to my parents in Switzerland. We'll contact them and see if it is time for us to move."

She sighed. "I know leaving is the best thing to do, but your grandfather built this factory. And my parents, they trust me to take care of them. How can I leave them?" She looked at him now with tears streaming down her face.

He took her into his arms. "You don't have to worry about your parents, they are taking matters into their own hands," he assured her, remembering their gazes of satisfaction as Frederick handed them the pills that his in-laws had begged him to obtain. "You know we have to leave as soon as possible." He felt her head nodding in agreement. "We will get through this."

"Ursula, breakfast is ready," the nanny called. "Coming," she replied. She placed her doll next to the others and commanded Hattie, "Now you make sure everyone stays out of trouble."

She skipped out of the room, still in her nightgown. On the way down the hallway she passed her parents' bedroom. She could see that some of her mother's jewelry lay on her dresser. Ursula could never resist trying on at least one piece of jewelry. As her eyes scanned the dresser she saw her favorite piece: a prism necklace—a long strand of prism-shaped crystal stones with gold edging. When

Ursula's mother wore it she would sometimes wrap it two or three times around her neck.

One day Mumma was sitting in a living room chair wearing the necklace. Ursula stood next to her.

"Mumma, I like your pretty necklace."

"Well, thank you, Ursula. It is beautiful, isn't it?"

Ursula nodded.

"And did you know that you can become as beautiful as this necklace?"

"Really?"

"Yes you can, as long as you listen." Mumma smiled. "Can you hear it?"

"Hear what?"

"Can you hear what the crystal prism necklace is saying?"

Ursula leaned in closer. "No, does it talk?"

"Oh, yes, loud and clear."

Ursula listened again. "Mumma, I don't hear anything." She frowned.

"But I hear it every day. Would you like me to tell you what it's saying?"

Ursula nodded in excitement, grinning broadly. Mumma unclasped the necklace and uncoiled it from around her neck. "The crystal prism tells us how to live. If you do what the crystal prism tells you, you will become as beautiful as the crystal prism."

She handed the long strand to Ursula.

"Now stand in front of the window and hold up the necklace."

She did as her mother requested. "Now look at the wall on the other side of the room."

Ursula turned her head to see a multitude of small rainbows.

"Isn't it beautiful?"

"Yes," Ursula smiled.

"As the light shines through, the beauty that is inside the crystal prism is shared with us. You are as beautiful as the crystal prism when you share with others."

"Really?" Ursula's eyes widened. She watched the small rainbows flitter.

"Yes! Look at the rainbows on the wall, aren't they colorful and bright?"

"Yes, they are so pretty."

"You are as colorful and bright as the prism rainbows when you smile and show kindness. Come here," she motioned to Ursula.

Ursula climbed onto her lap, carefully holding the necklace. Mumma held out her hand and Ursula gave it to her.

"Now Ursula, I want you to feel one side of the stone," said Mumma.

Ursula ran her finger over it.

"Now the other side."

Ursula felt the opposite side.

"Do you see how one side is rough and the other side is smooth?"

"Yes."

"The crystal prism is telling you to think positive thoughts. For every rough, bad day that you have, you will have a smooth, good one. Do you feel how hard and strong the stone is?"

Ursula watched Mumma put one of the crystals

between two of her fingers and squeeze. Ursula squeezed a stone as well.

Mumma nodded. "You will become as strong as the crystal prism when you keep a promise that you make. Now one last thing, I want you to put the crystal prism to your eye and look through it. What do you see?"

Ursula looked at Mumma through the stone. "Oh, I see lots of little yous!"

Mumma laughed. "But there's only one me, and you are seeing more than one me, right?"

"Yes," she exclaimed excitedly.

"The crystal prism is telling you to keep an open mind because there's always more than one way to look at something."

Ursula put the necklace down, pondering all that Mumma had said.

"Ursula I know this is a lot to understand, but it's very important. Do you want to know why it's important?"

"Yes."

"Good! Stand up."

Ursula stood, and Mumma handed her the necklace.

"Hold the necklace up as high as you can."

Ursula stretched her arm up as far as she could. The necklace was so long that it almost touched the floor.

"See how long the necklace is?"

"Yes."

"The necklace is saying that if you follow all of the crystal prism principles, you will have a long, happy life."

Ursula laughed and jumped back onto her mother's lap. Mumma hugged her.

"I know this is a lot to remember, but will you try?"

"I will try, Mumma."

Long, happy life, Ursula thought as she held up the necklace. Ursula mimicked her mother and wrapped it several times around her neck, then paraded around the room. She pretended she was an adult.

"Oh, yes sir. I would love to go to a dinner party with you," she said, talking to her image in the mirror. She curtsied.

"Ursula, are you coming?" the nanny called again.

"Oops." Nanny's voice startled her, waking her from her daydream. She unwrapped the crystal necklace from around her neck and laid it gently back on her mother's dresser. She walked down the stairs, inhaling the sweet cinnamon aroma wafting upwards. Nanny made porridge, she thought. As she neared the bottom of the steps she could hear her two-year-old brother, Little Hanrie, approach from the front room. *It sure would be fun to scare him,* she thought. And she knew the perfect hiding place. Scurrying into the dining room, she knew Little Hanrie would have to pass past her to get to the kitchen where breakfast was waiting. In there she spied her lair, the curtains.

The dark, green velvet curtains hung majestically from ceiling to floor on the one large dining room window. The curtains were so thick and heavy that it wasn't even until last year that Ursula was strong enough to move them. She was smug with confidence knowing that Hanrie could not move them. She hid behind them, trying to be quiet. Her little body wiggled nervously. *Oh, hurry Hanrie,* she thought. Just as she felt she could not stand the anticipation any longer she heard his approaching footsteps and his mumbled toddler gibberish.

"Boo!" Ursula yelled as she jumped out from behind the curtains. Bleary-eyed Little Hanrie jumped in surprise as his bottom lip started to quiver. Ursula laughed. Hanrie blinked and rubbed his eyes. He saw it was Ursula and smiled broadly. She grabbed his hand and they ran into the kitchen together.

"Finally!" the nanny exclaimed. "Now everyone, please eat. We have lots to do today."

All the five Swartz children sat at the kitchen table eating their eggs and porridge. Hilda was the oldest and even at the age of sixteen, one could see the beginning signs of a beautiful woman emerging. As a result, she had many young men pleading for her company.

To her father's delight, Hilda played the violin. She started taking lessons when she was eight years old, and had become quite good. Frequently, after dinner, the family would gather in the front room and Hilda and Poppa would play their violins. Mumma would accompany them on the piano. Ursula fondly remembered the musical nights as though they were a distant dream.

"Ladies and Gentlemen, presenting the Swartz family," one would declare. Ursula or her older brother, Ludwig, would stand on the ottoman with their hands cupped together in front of their mouths as a pretend megaphone. They'd clap and the musicians would bow and curtsy. Then they would start to play. Sometimes the music — slow and soothing — would put Ursula and Little Hanrie to sleep. Other times they would be on their feet dancing and singing.

Then there came a time when these joyful concerts didn't seem to happen as often as before. Ursula wasn't sure why, and it saddened her. Was it because Hilda preferred dating to playing the violin? Little did Ursula comprehend the anxiety concerning the threatening and growing presence of Nazi soldiers in the little town of Glashütte. Whatever the reason, Ursula wished the dancing and singing would return. *Maybe Sophus will bring it back,* she thought.

Ten-year-old Sophus Swartz was being taught to play the piano by Mumma. As Mumma would guide her fingers along the keys, Sophus' head would bob up and down making her dark brown curls bounce animatedly like tiny marionettes. Mumma would compliment Sophus for doing so well with her piano lessons and Sophus would smile. And when Sophus smiled one could not help but feel fortunate to be near her. Her teeth shone like perfect pearls through her rosy pink lips and coupled with her large brown doe eyes it seemed like all of heaven could be found in her face. She was a quiet girl with a cheerful disposition and made friends quite easily. Ursula thought that maybe Hilda was a little jealous of Sophus' beauty, and that was why she always complained about her, even now...

"No, I don't want to take Sophus to the library with me," Hilda said viciously to Nanny's request.

Sophus sorrowfully gazed at her porridge, swirling her spoon mindlessly.

Hilda doesn't want Sophus to smile, Ursula thought. Hilda knew that if she took Sophus with her to the library that any young man's attention would not be totally hers.

Ludwig, sitting next to Sophus, gently nudged her arm.

"Don't worry Sophus, you can come to the park with me. We'll have lots of fun."

Sophus raised her head and looked at Ludwig. She smiled. Ludwig snarled at Hilda and she responded by sticking out her tongue at him.

"Stop it now! Look at what you are teaching the younger ones," Nanny cried, and pointed to Hanrie, who was now sticking out his cereal-plastered tongue to everyone.

"Sorry, Nan," said Ludwig apologetically.

Ludwig tried hard not to laugh at Hanrie. He knew Nanny was right; he had to be the good example. He was the eldest boy in the family and even though he was four years younger than Hilda, he felt intellectually superior to her. He read and studied constantly and had a gift for understanding foreign languages. His physical charac-teristics were similar to Ursula's and because of that she felt they had a special bond. "Us redheads have to stick together," he had once said to her after he had saved her from a teasing playmate.

Ursula was very proud of her older brother and loved him very much.

And then there sat Ursula, fidgeting in her chair — impulsive, exuberant and lovable, all rolled into one little fireball. Ursula's life consisted of obeying Nanny, attending her ballet lessons and playing with her little brother. She watched her little brother now as he sat in his highchair. His face was covered with the porridge that he was trying desperately to get into his mouth.

Oh Hanrie, you're such a little mess, she thought. They had so much fun together. Ursula could not imagine a day without him.

Little Hanrie looked at her and smiled, seeming to know her thoughts.

"Nanny, do I have a ballet lesson today?"

"Yes, you do. And it's early today, so let's hop to it."

"Do you remember when I danced in the Spring Recital?"

"How could we forget?" Hilda interrupted. "You talked about it for two months."

"Hilda," Nanny scolded. "Yes I do, and you did a wonderful job."

"They said there was an important man in the audience, but I don't remember his name. Do you remember?" Ursula asked.

"That was Hitler, pumpkin," Nanny replied.

The mention of his name drew groans from Hilda and Ludwig.

Ludwig laid down his spoon and shoved the bowl away. "Well, I've just lost my appetite. Are you ready to go Sophus?"

Sophus nodded and consumed her last bite of food. They dabbed their mouths with their napkins and excused themselves from the table.

"I'm ready to go too," Hilda announced.

"Okay everybody, don't forget to put on your armbands and be back here at noon," Nanny commanded.

They all shouted back their polite affirmations and after a few moments of noisy commotion and banging doors, all became silent in the Swartz home.

"Bye!" Little Hanrie yelled.

Nanny and Ursula laughed.

"After we get this mess and this little guy cleaned up,"

she said while stroking the small tuft of brown hair on Hanrie's head, "we'll take you to your ballet lesson."

Ursula smiled. She helped Nanny to clear the dishes from the table. After Nanny had cleaned Hanrie's face and changed him into fresh clothing, Ursula and Hanrie went into their playroom. Hanrie drew some of his wooden cars out of the toy box and started playing. He made motor sounds as he pushed them along the floor.

Ursula could hear the water running in the kitchen as Nanny washed the dishes. The sweet scent of the soapy water wafted into the playroom. For a few seconds Ursula stood watching Hanrie and listening to the soothing sounds of the water. These familiar sounds and scents encircled her…engulfed her…entranced her. At that moment, Ursula was content.

Chapter Two

It was late summer and the heat felt like a huge hand pressing downward, hindering every limb's movement and every inhaled breath. But the oppressive heat seemed to have no influence on Ursula. She was skipping joyfully in her tutu.

"Ursula slow down," complained Hilda. Unlike Ursula, Hilda did mind the heat. It made her curly, black hair kinky, and she hoped she would not be seen by any single young gentlemen. Hilda trudged along wishing that she had not been the one to take Ursula home from her ballet class. *I even have to carry her ballet slippers,* Hilda grumbled. She watched Ursula skipping in front of her. Her pink tutu bobbed up and down in rhythm to her ponytail. Hilda smiled. *She is a funny little thing,* she thought. Shifting her eyes to Ursula's arm, she spotted the black armband. Any feeling of joy that that moment had allowed her dispersed. She felt her own armband snug around her bicep.

Hilda had always been proud of her heritage, and when the ordinance first went into effect she didn't mind wearing the armband. In fact, she wore it like a badge of honor. But one day as she was walking home from school wearing it, a German woman, a stranger to Hilda, came up to her. She yelled obscenities at Hilda and then spat on her. Hilda ran home crying the whole way.

Why did she do that? I didn't do anything to her, she thought. With her pride trampled, she felt dirty and degraded.

They were just a few houses away from home now. Hilda looked at her watch and breathed a sigh of relief. They were going to be home long before curfew time. Hilda knew how important it was to follow the ordinances put into place by the SS. She had watched many families being taken forcibly from their homes and imagined it was because they had broken the rules. In front of her, Ursula bounded up the steps.

Ursula tried desperately to turn the knob, first with one hand then two, but couldn't because of her sweaty palms. "Hilda come on!" she stamped her foot anxiously.

Hilda reached the front steps with her usual smirk of annoyance, and opened the door for Ursula. As they stepped into the foyer, they could hear Sophus practicing on the piano. Ursula could also hear the faint sound of sloshing water coming from the room just beyond the kitchen where Nanny was washing laundry.

Hanrie came up to greet Ursula and Hilda with a squeal of delight. Ursula hugged him. Then they went into the living room where they found Poppa sitting in his chair reading the newspaper and Ludwig laying on the floor reading a book. Mumma was sitting on the piano bench with Sophus.

"Mumma," Ursula interrupted excitedly, "watch what I learned today." With outstretched arms she pointed her toe and slid it to the front of her and then to the back.

Hilda stood in the archway between the hallway and living room and rolled her eyes. Mumma and Sophus smiled and clapped. Poppa laid his newspaper on his lap and clapped too. Ludwig smiled.

"That is wonderful, Ursula," said Mumma.

"Urshey," Sophus said, "you can do that while I play."

Ursula was thrilled. *Oh, yes! Beautiful Sophus, I knew you would bring the singing and the dancing back. I'll do anything for you, Sophus, just to see you smile.* Ursula held her arms out.

"Wait for me," insisted Poppa. He walked over to the fireplace and grabbed his violin and bow from the mantle. He placed the violin on his arm, nodded to Ursula and nestled his chin on the chin rest. She, in turn, nodded to Sophus, who positioned her fingers for the first notes.

Ludwig jumped up onto the ottoman. "Introducing, the Swartz's!" he dramatically announced, and then jumped down. He and Hanrie clapped. Then Sophus began playing.

It was aurally painful at first. Sophus would accidentally hit two keys at once or play the wrong note. But slowly her confidence built and a familiar tune emerged. Poppa gingerly stroked the strings, not wanting to distract Sophus. Slowly the two harmonized, then Ursula began.

Her legs seemed weightless as she moved them in perfect timing, in perfect form. Her mother and father swayed to the melody. Ludwig smiled and watched Ursula. Hilda sat cross-legged on a chair combing her hair with her fingers. Little Hanrie lay across the ottoman, swinging his legs and sucking on his pacifier.

Suddenly Ursula felt herself caught up in a warm euphoric wave and felt slightly dizzy. She didn't understand the emotion she was feeling and it frightened her. Should she stop dancing? *No,* she thought, *this must not stop!* She continued, and now the room was spinning and she was floating and Sophus was smiling and everyone and everything was warm and happy. Then came a knock on the door.

Initially no one heard the knock on the front door until it became a pounding fist. The music and the spinning room came to a stop. Mr. Swartz laid his violin back on the mantle. He and Ludwig went to the front door. Hilda picked up Hanrie. Mumma stood up and Ursula and Sophus swarmed around her. The pounding persisted.

Suddenly, Ursula felt fearful. *Who could it be? Mumma and Poppa aren't expecting anyone.*

As soon as Mr. Swartz turned the knob, armed SS soldiers stampeded into the house. They held up their rifles, pointing at all the members of the Swartz family.

Ludwig grabbed his father's arm. Sophus and Ursula started to cry and Hilda held Hanrie's head closer to hers. Then one man swaggered inside, his head cocked with a domineering sneer — obviously the officer in command.

"Where is Mrs. Swartz?" he demanded, surveying those at gunpoint.

"I am here," she said. She pried her children's arms from around her and stepped forward.

Frederick shook his head begging her to be quiet. *If it's me they want,* she thought, *maybe they will let everyone else go.*

The officer in command stepped toward her. At that moment they heard the back door slam, a woman scream, then a gunshot.

"Nanny!" Sophus gasped. The officer walked over to Sophus. He put his hand under her chin and lifted her face to meet his. She blinked, and her tears rolled down her face and onto his hand.

"Aw, pretty one, Nanny should not have tried to leave." He let go of her chin and patted her head. He nodded to one of the soldiers while pointing to Sophus. The soldier nodded in return. He turned to Mrs. Swartz.

"It seems you are a very bad accountant." He slapped her hard across her face, reddening her cheek immediately.

"Wait!" yelled Frederick as he pushed Ludwig away from him.

Three soldiers quickly attacked Mr. Swartz. They used

the butts of their rifles and bludgeoned various parts of his body. It was the blow to his head that knocked him to the floor. He lay there moaning at Ludwig's feet.

The commanding officer came over and kneeled down at Mr. Swartz's side. Frederick could vaguely see him through the sweat and blood that was dripping into his eyes.

"I don't need any help in disciplining your wife, Mr. Swartz," he chuckled. He touched his finger to a pool of blood at Frederick's temple and swiped it down his face. "In fact maybe you can learn something from me."

"Go to hell," Frederick managed to mutter through swelling lips as the officer stood up.

"You have an interest in hell, Mr. Swartz? Good, because that is where you and your family are going."

The German officer then kicked Frederick in his side.

"Listen everyone, we are going for a ride!" he yelled at the Swartz family. He turned to his men. "Take them all out to the truck."

The soldiers rushed forward. Several of them dragged Mr. Swartz along the floor. The other men grabbed the children by their arms. Mumma noticed that Ursula was still in her tutu. She was afraid to speak, but she knew she had to.

"Please, sir," Mumma asked, trembling, "can my daughter change her clothes?" He looked at Anna with disgust and then at Ursula. He grabbed Ursula's arm and pushed her toward the steps. She held on to the banister.

"All right, but hurry up!" he screamed at Ursula. Ursula fearfully looked back at Mumma. She watched as all the members of her family were prodded out the door.

"It's okay, Urshey, go up and change," Mumma pleaded.

Tears cascaded down Mumma's cheeks. It scared Ursula. She had never seen Mumma cry. Ursula ran up the steps to her room, her heart pounding. There she hastily undressed, poking a hole in the tutu's crinoline. Once naked, she stood there trembling, looking into her open closet. She picked a green dress that she hated; she didn't want to look nice for the mean man who had pushed her onto the steps. Also the dress rested two inches below her knee and had deep generous pockets that she thought may be a helpful attribute. She put on her shoes and noticed her favorite doll, Hattie, sitting at the foot of her bed. She grabbed her doll and started down the hallway. Passing her parents' bedroom she saw the crystal prism necklace lying on Mumma's dresser. She picked it up and slid it into her dress pocket. *Mumma may need this later*, she thought. She walked to the steps.

Perched on the landing, she listened. The house was silent. *They left without me.* She felt scared, yet relieved. She stepped cautiously, down...down...watching, listening. With her foot on the last step, she froze. She heard the soldiers outside, yelling and banging doors. *I have to hide! The curtains! They'll never find me there!*

She ran into the dining room and dashed behind the curtains. Her heart was pounding and her lungs felt as though they were on fire. She tried to make her breaths shallow and to hold her frightened, trembling body still. *These curtains are so thick and heavy, they will never find me here.*

She looked out the window and noticed the sky was reddening. She made every muscle in her body tight so she couldn't move. She felt safe. *I wonder how long I will need to stay here. Where are Mumma and Poppa going? Will I ever see them again?*

She noticed an airplane high up in the sky and saw a big black bird effortlessly floating with the wind. How she wished she was that bird. How she wished her whole family were birds. *We'd fly away from those mean men.*

Contemplating her flight, she didn't hear the footsteps.

"Aha," yelled the Nazi soldier as he tore open the curtain. Ursula screamed. The soldier grabbed her arm and pulled her out of her hiding place. He wrenched the doll from her arms and threw it at the wall. A small piece of porcelain from Hattie's face flew into the air.

"No!" Ursula yelled.

The anger welled up inside of her. She spied his unconcealed flesh and bit into his hand. He screamed and then smacked her hard with his free hand. She was knocked to the floor.

"Why, you vermin brat!" he roared. He reached for his gun. "I could kill you right now and no one would care!" He dropped his hand slowly to his side. "No, I won't kill you now. I'm going to enjoy watching you suffer." He then forcibly lifted her up, pulling her down the hallway and out the door to the awaiting vehicle.

The military truck had a roof over the back and the tailgate was down. Ursula looked in and saw many people crammed into the small compartment. Some were sitting, some standing, but all wore lurid, frightened faces. She saw Mumma sitting. Mumma held out her arms and the soldier put Ursula on Mumma's lap. Hilda was sitting next to Mumma with Hanrie on her lap. Next to her, Ludwig and Hilda sat on opposite sides of Poppa helping him to stay upright. Sophus clung to Ludwig's other arm.

"I found her hiding behind some curtains and she gave me quite a fight. She's a feisty one," the soldier said, staring angrily at Ursula.

"We'll get that out of her," another soldier teased.

They laughed as they lifted the tailgate. They then jumped onto the fenders and one of them whistled. The idling truck lurched into gear. As they drove away Ursula watched their house dwindle. In the sky she could still see the big, black bird. Then Ursula remembered what the tall, gruff officer had said.

"Mumma, how far is it to hell?"

Mumma didn't answer. She just closed her eyes and laid her head on Ursula's. They were silent the rest of the ride to the train station. Every now and then Ursula could feel a warm, wet tear fall onto her head.

Chapter Three

It was dark when the truck arrived at the train station. Ursula peeked outside, and by the light of the lampposts she could see that there were several military trucks, much like the one she was in, pulling into the train station as well. She saw into the back of one of the trucks and noticed that it was also full of people. She also noticed that Nazi soldiers had positioned themselves along the train track, seemingly awaiting their arrival. They bore rifles and flashlights and held tightly onto barking German Shepherds pulling at their leashes.

She watched as the truck stopped in front of the track and as soldiers surrounded it. To Ursula it seemed as if the soldiers had appeared out of nowhere, multiplying before her eyes. They yelled to the people inside the truck, pointing their rifles at them. The dogs lunged toward the back of the truck, barking and snarling.

The people came out reluctantly and were pushed toward the open train cars. As they entered the boxcars, Ursula could hear them screaming and crying. Then the truck carrying the Swartz family swerved and came to a stop. It was now their turn.

Immediately the soldiers swarmed the truck, hastily throwing the tailgate down. Mumma and Ursula exited the truck first, followed by the rest of the family. Then everyone else in the truck climbed down. Little Hanrie was crying and patting his belly. He had been fast asleep in Hilda's arms, but the barking dogs and his growling stomach had awakened him.

The SS soldiers formed a line from the truck to the train. They pointed to the open boxcar and pushed the people toward it. "Hurry, hurry!" they yelled.

As the Jews approached the boxcar they smelled a horrendous odor of excrement and vomit. The Swartzes stopped in disgust, covering their mouths and noses. A soldier fired his rifle at the ground close to their feet. "Get in now or die here!"

The children cried.

"Shh, it's okay my darlings," Anna said. She peered inside, but could see only a small section of the boxcar that was dimly lit by the surrounding lampposts. "Now, everyone, grab someone else's hand and we'll walk in together."

"I'm going in first," Frederick demanded. He limped to the head of the line and held his hand out to Ursula. She grabbed it. Anna walked quickly over to Hilda. She took Hanrie from her arms and took hold of Hilda's hand. Ludwig and Sophus joined hands with them, and they all started their way into the boxcar.

Frederick walked into the darkness slowly and carefully, with his outstretched hand feeling his way along the side of the boxcar's wooden slats. He became submerged in the stale air, drowning in the boxcar's fetid darkness. The putrid smell was worse than anything he had ever known. It filled his nostrils and instantly permeated his body. He swallowed hard trying to keep his stomach contents down. Behind him, Frederick heard people screaming and crying as they were pushed into the boxcar. The soldiers yelled. Gunshots were fired intermittently. The dogs barked incessantly. Frederick pressed forward, holding the only thing that was real for him at that moment — Ursula's tiny hand.

Holding tightly onto her father, Ursula stepped into a puddle and then into something soft and squishy. She winced. They reached the back of the boxcar. Frederick let out a deep sigh. "Now, everyone, say your names, I want to know you're okay." They replied. Frederick felt relieved. Then Ursula spoke.

"But, Poppa, Hanrie can't say his name." He wanted to laugh; he wanted to pick her up, pick them all up, and whisk his whole family away. He wanted to wake up from this nightmare, but all he had the strength to do was to hold her hand tighter.

As people flooded in, the Swartz family was squeezed further into the corner of the boxcar. Then more people were forced into the car and the Swartz family was squished together even more. Then more people were forced inside, pressing, pushing. When at last the Nazis were convinced that not one more person could fit in the boxcar, the door was slammed shut and the meager light that shone in from the lampposts was gone. In the abject darkness, they huddled together listening to the same scenario in the next boxcar.

"I'm scared Poppa," Ursula said.

"Oh, Urshey," he let go of her hand and laid his hand gently on the side of her head, drawing her nearer to him. "You must try to be brave, like a tiger."

Little Hanrie was crying. Ursula wondered if it was due to his hunger or the darkness.

They stood there for a while longer, waiting and listening. Then the last boxcar door shut. The scream of the train whistle then shook the night, echoing the wailing of those held inside. Suddenly, their boxcar lunged into movement and began wobbling its way down the track.

Questions whirled around in Ursula's mind, but the screeching sound of metal wheels against metal track was deafening, making conversation impossible. Ursula wrapped her arm around Poppa's leg.

As the train continued to build speed, Ursula desperately wanted to see her surroundings. Tiny pinpoints of light flashed sporadically through the holes in the sides of the boxcar, but the light mocked her, allowing her to catch a glimpse only every so often. And with every glimpse that the mocking light allowed her to see, all she beheld was the same sorrowful face on a different body.

As her body grew tired and she struggled to keep her eyes open, Ursula felt herself drifting off to sleep. But then a flash of light shone in front of her and she saw just inches from her face the face of a demon! She gasped. Darkness. Another flash of light and she saw Sophus turning her head to face her. *It was just Sophus' hair!* Her thoughts spun in her head until finally, within the droning of the train, she let herself fall asleep on Poppa's leg.

Hours passed. The sun began rising. Ursula awakened. Everything was as before—the screeching of metal, the wobbling of the boxcar, except now there was an even shimmer of morning light that peeked its way through the wooden slats. Her arm was still secure around Poppa's leg, and she could see her family standing close to her. Hilda was in the corner of the boxcar, where she took advantage of the walls to hold herself up. Sophus and Ludwig leaned against Mumma on either side of her. Dread and gloom lurked in every face that she could see. She had been standing for so long that her feet tingled with pain. She wished that she could sit, but she looked down and there at her feet was Hanrie. All the members of the family had made a small circle around him and he lay across everyone's feet, sleeping.

As the train rattled onward, a melancholy droan permeated the air. Ursula watched the dust particles that floated about their confined space. She imagined the particles to be tiny ballerinas—dancing, whirling, performing pirouettes for her.

More hours passed and then the train came to a stop. The doors of their boxcar opened and the Nazis, screaming and yelling, forced everyone out. Stiff and numb, the Jews exited, stumbling onto the stones beside the track, squinting their eyes at the direct sunlight. The soldiers then pushed them from the stones onto a dirt path where they joined other somber Jews.

Mumma picked up Hanrie. He cried in Mumma's arms, rubbing his stomach. Sophus and Ludwig walked together. Ursula took Poppa and Hilda's hands and walked with them toward the open boxcar door. They had been the first to enter and were now the last to leave; or at least Ursula thought they were the last. As she turned to go out the door she looked behind her. In the back of the boxcar, on the other side of where her family had been, there lay an old man groaning. Ursula became concerned.

"Poppa, is that man hurt?"

He turned his head to see what Ursula was referring to, but before he could respond two Nazi soldiers jumped into the boxcar, pushing them outside. As Ursula stepped onto the stones, she heard a gunshot from inside. Her mouth opened in horror and she looked up at her father. For a split second he had the same expression of terror on his face, but he knew he had to be brave for her.

"Urshey, we must be strong. Remember: tiger." He curled his top lip, "Grr."

She nodded as they joined the rest of the Jews walking the dirt path. The soldiers commanded them to be silent, pointing their rifles in the direction they were to walk. The soldiers barked commands. Their dogs barked just as viciously, baring their teeth and dripping saliva. They plodded along mile after mile, unable to speak, under a submissive cloud of fear. Fatigue and hunger battled against their bodies, yet they continued walking for fear of being shot. *How much longer must we walk?* Ursula questioned silently as her small body ached with every step.

Finally, on their right, they came upon a tall barbed-wire fence that surrounded a compound. Buildings and a fog of dust obstructed her view, but Ursula could hear all sorts of commotion coming from the other side. *Where are we?* she wondered.

Her question was answered as the path made a slight turn and she saw the sign next to the entranceway: "Bergen-Belsen."

Chapter Four

They stepped through the entranceway into the concentration camp known as Bergen-Belsen. Even though it was summertime, a chill stabbed at Ursula's legs. She gazed up at Poppa and Hilda and a dreadful thought stung her mind: *Could this be hell?*

The large company of Jews was led into a holding area. Ursula turned to look into the compound. She saw many massive buildings. The ground was barren and dry with little sign of vegetative life. Yet there was life, a deceptive life of groaning and movement. Gray figures moved about slowly, lethargically, like moving statues. Ursula could see other grayish figures sitting and lying around. There were indiscernible heaps haphazardly plopped here and there. Ursula gazed intently, trying to see what comprised the mounds. Suddenly, Ursula's gaze was blocked by a row of Nazi soldiers holding onto the leashes of vicious dogs. As the Nazis closed the gates of the holding pen, the hinges screeched loudly and the latch clanked, as if howling the Jews' impending, sadistic doom. *Are these the gates of hell?* Ursula fearfully wondered.

On opposite sides of the holding area were two huge buildings. A metal card table sat in the farthest right corner of the holding pen, next to one of the buildings. Several chairs were placed behind it. Then, all at once, as if orchestrated by an invisible conductor, standing soldiers sprang into action.

"Get in line!," they yelled at the confused, tired people. Other Nazi soldiers came into the holding area and began pushing the Jews into a line against the fence.

Ursula heard some people sobbing.

"Quiet!" the Nazis yelled as they walked up and down the line, leering at the Jews. One soldier stopped abruptly as he noticed something shiny on Frederick's wrist. He picked up Poppa's arm and admired his watch, the gold watch with diamonds on its dial that Mumma had given him as a gift. There was never a time that Ursula could remember that he had not worn it. The Nazi became engrossed with the watch, turning Frederick's hand to examine the clasp.

"Attention!" someone yelled. The soldier dropped Poppa's arm. "*Heil, Hitler!*" the Nazis exclaimed, thrusting their arms upward as the commanding officer strode into the pen. He was carrying a large book. He resounded the soldiers' "*Heil Hitler*" and then spoke to the frightened Jews.

"You are now in a facility where you will be for an undetermined length of time. If you obey our orders no harm will come to you. You will be given a hot meal, but first we need some information."

He walked over to the table, sat down on one of the chairs behind it, and opened the large book. A soldier stood next to the officer, and as he offered his pen to the commander, Ursula noticed a bandage wrapped around his hand. It was the same man that she had bitten! Terrified, Ursula clung to Poppa's arm and swallowed hard. After turning several pages, the officer summoned the soldiers to bring people to the table.

One by one, families were ushered to the table by an armed soldier. After a brief talk the officer wrote something in his book and the family was taken aside. The soldier who had admired Poppa's watch nudged Poppa's arm, shoving him in the direction of the table. The Swartz family apprehensively approached.

"State your names starting with the father and mother." The commanding officer looked up from his book. Ursula kept her head down, hoping that the standing soldier would not recognize her.

"Frederick and Anna Swartz and our children, Hilda, Ludwig, Sophus, Ursula and Hanrie," stated Frederick. He felt a deep sense of shame as if he had given his family over to a certain evil fate. The officer smiled as he noticed the cuts and bruises on Frederick's face.

"Well, I see you know how important it is that you cooperate," the officer snickered.

Frederick didn't move.

"Swartz," he started writing in the book. "Did you own any property?"

"Yes we did," he answered listlessly.

"Swartz," he tapped his pen on his head. "Ah, yes, the doll factory."

"Toy factory," he corrected him, lowering his eyes.

The officer grinned maliciously, turning the book around so that the lines faced Frederick.

"Doll, toy, call it what you like. Sign here," he said as he lay the pen down for Frederick.

Frederick's hand shook uncontrollably as he reached for the pen. His body shivered as he picked it up. He hesitated and sighed loudly.

The commanding officer's eyes met Frederick's. Like venom from a snake, Frederick was stabbed by the cold hatred in his eyes. It jolted him, shrinking him. The officer stood up quickly, pulled his gun out from its' holster and pointed the gun at Frederick's head.

"Don't try my patience any longer, Mr. Swartz! Sign or your children will watch you die!"

The officer stood for a few moments, until Frederick lowered his eyes. Putting his gun back into the holster, he sat down and pointed to the book. "You sign on this line and Mrs. Swartz here. Now hurry!"

As Frederick acceded to the officer's demands, the officer's attention turned to the children.

He looked at Hilda first, his eyes noticeably traveling up and down her body. He winked at her and she smiled shyly. He nodded affirmatively at Ludwig, and then his eye caught Sophus. He grinned widely, hungrily. "And what is your name?"

"So-So-Sophus," she stuttered.

"Sophus? No need to be afraid my little one. How old are you, twelve?"

"Ten," interrupted Anna defensively, holding onto Hanrie tighter.

"Mr. Swartz!" His face turned red as he yelled. "Can

you not control that woman?" He slammed his fist on the rickety table, making it wobble.

Ursula flinched, attracting the attention of the standing soldier. Suddenly, the soldier's head dropped down to her level. She could feel his eyes examining her. She grew increasingly uneasy and in an uncontrollable instant her eyes glanced upward to meet his. She could see the spark of recognition in his eyes and fear welled up inside her yet again. The soldier spoke into the officer's ear. The commander shook his head and then looked at Ursula. He looked again at his comrade's wounded hand and then at Ursula. She watched as he rose from his seat, seeming to her to become bigger and more frightful than any man she had ever seen before. His eyes bulged from their sockets as his face turned purple. "Get them away from me!" he screamed.

The soldiers responded immediately. They pulled the Swartz family away from the table and threw them into the fence on the opposite side of the holding pen. There they sat down on the ground and huddled together. Hanrie sobbed on Mumma's shoulder while Hilda rubbed his back trying to comfort him. Ludwig, Sophus and Ursula clustered around Poppa. A soldier stood near them with his growling German Shepherd, guarding them. They waited, afraid to move, and watched the rest of the families in the line take their turn at the table.

The last family was eventually led away from the table while the commanding officer finished writing in his book. He slammed it shut, saluted the soldiers and left the pen carrying the book. Ursula cowered as he passed, hoping he would not punish her. The remaining soldiers acted quickly, forcing those who were sitting to stand and those who were standing to move. They started to divide the people into groups. A few Nazis opened the large doors of both buildings at the opposite ends of the holding area.

"Women and children in the building on the right, men and boys twelve years and older in the building on the left," they ordered.

The people cried and pleaded, not wanting to be separated from their loved ones. They held on to each other fervently. Some soldiers appeared to be sympathetic. A young soldier walked over to Hilda and put his hand on her shoulder. Then he spoke to the crowd.

"You will not be hurt. You are going to change into your new uniforms. You will come out and see your family again." He looked at Hilda and smiled, patting her shoulder lightly.

His words appeased the crowd, so they split their families by age and gender as they were commanded. The soldiers forced them into lines and then marched them at gunpoint into the appropriate building. Ursula looked over and waved to Poppa and Ludwig as she neared the doorway. As Poppa waved, his gold watch glinted in the sunlight.

When the line of women and children were inside the building, the doors were shut. A long wooden bench leaned against the whole length of the right side. Ursula noticed at the far end of the building's interior a concrete block wall with openings on both sides. "Stay in line! Keep walking!" they shouted. The Nazis pushed the Jews. "Hurry!"

On the left side chairs were lined up on the concrete floor. Electrical cords hung on the wall behind them and a large metal table was positioned next to the concrete block wall. The Nazi soldiers scurried around plugging razors into the outlets as other soldiers armed with rifles walked up and down the line of people intimidating them.

"Quiet!" they yelled.

"Mumma, what are they going to do with those razors?" panicked Hilda.

Anna sighed and apathetically answered, "It will grow back."

"No, Mumma, please," Hilda protested.

Anna knew there was no point in protesting or in comforting. The inevitable was to occur. They were taken to a place where time had ceased and hope no longer existed. Starting with one end of the line, the armed soldiers pointed and commanded the Jews to come over and sit in the chairs. They showed no pity as they ran the razors over their heads. Some people cried as their locks of hair fell to the ground.

Anna looked at her children. "We will not cry. We will show them how strong we are. Do you understand?"

The children nodded yes, but tears were already making their wet paths down Sophus' cheeks.

Anna wiped her tears. "No, my dear, you will be strong."

Sophus nodded again. The armed soldiers came toward them and pointed for Ursula and Hilda to sit in two empty chairs. Anna noticed that the one man held Hilda's arm and spoke into her ear as they walked. Ursula and Hilda sat down. The razors were turned on and the men standing behind the girls started shaving. The man cutting Ursula's hair accidentally jabbed her scalp with the razor.

"Ouch," she cried out.

The soldiers responded with roars of laughter. She sat defiantly still, her lips twisted in anger. He started cutting again. He was still chuckling when he jabbed her again. She sat still holding her hands tightly in her lap.

No, I will not cry. She did not think that this time was an accident, nor the next time, or the time after that, until finally it was over and the soldier behind her pushed her out of the chair. She held her throbbing scalp and looked up at her barber with hatred in her eyes. He was smacking the razor on his palm freeing the last strands of Ursula's red hair from the blades. He scowled at her. The other Nazi had finished Hilda and she walked over to Ursula, shamefully covering her shaved head with her hands.

Sophus and Mumma with Little Hanrie in her arms were then directed to the chairs. Sophus sat in the same chair that Ursula had.

Oh, please don't cry, Sophus, Ursula wished silently. Ursula stood close and watched. Sophus bit her lower lip and closed her eyes as the man began to cut. To Ursula's surprise the man didn't jab Sophus. In fact, he seemed to be caressing her head with the razor, and when he was finished, he smiled.

In the other chair Mumma held Hanrie on her lap. The SS soldier had finished shaving her hair off and now he was attempting to cut Hanrie's. Hanrie screamed and fidgeted as the razor touched his head. The Nazi fumed. "If you cannot shut him up I will just cut off his head!"

"Shh," Anna whispered to Hanrie. The razor frightened him. Hanrie's hair grew in a scant clump on the top of his head and Anna never had the need to cut it. She held him close, clamping his body with her legs and holding his head still with one hand on each side of his head. The cutting continued while Little Hanrie fussed. When the razor stopped, Hanrie felt his head in wonderment and looked at Mumma. He was still crying. She hugged him, rocking slowly.

"That's enough," the soldier yelled harshly. "Get back in line!"

Anna stood and gathered her children. As they walked over to the other side of the building, Little Hanrie whined and patted his stomach.

"I know you're hungry, Hanrie," Anna stroked his head. She spoke to all of her children, "We will get food soon." Or at least she hoped so. She could feel her own body shaking with hunger. She knew her children had to be feeling the same.

When the soldiers were satisfied that all the people were back on the other side of the building, they commanded the Jews to unclothe. "Undress," the soldiers instructed. "Get undressed!"

"What?" a woman replied incredulously. Her reply caught a soldier's attention. He barrelled toward her pulling out his gun and stopped directly in front of her.

"Undress now!" he screamed, the gun just inches from her face.

With her hands shaking, she began to unbutton her blouse. The soldier paced up and down the line frantically, pointing his rifle at everyone. "Now! Now!" he kept shouting.

The people wept as they undressed.

"Mumma, I'm scared," fretted Hilda. Sophus was clinging to Hilda's arm, sobbing and shaking in agreement. Mumma set Hanrie down on the floor next to Ursula. She placed her hands firmly on their shoulders.

"I'm scared, too. But it's best if we do what they want, quickly."

Hilda and Sophus surrendered, and as their clothes fell to the floor they tried sheepishly to cover their nakedness. They sat on the bench, hugging each other, hiding each other. The soldiers watched and laughed, pointing at the women as they disrobed.

While Mumma undressed, Ursula helped Hanrie. When Mumma was unclad, Ursula looked up at her. She gestured for Mumma to lean down.

"Mumma, I have something in my pocket. I don't want them to see it," she whispered into her ear.

Anna lifted her eyebrows. She turned her back to the soldiers and squatted down pretending to help Ursula unclothe. She peeked around cautiously then put her hand into Ursula's pocket and felt the necklace. She couldn't believe it. Pulling it out just a little bit so she could see it, she looked at Ursula in astonishment.

"Are you mad, Mumma?"

"Oh no, my dear child," the tears welled up in her eyes.

"I brought it for you, Mumma. I thought you might need to see things in a different way."

"Oh, Urshey," she hugged her tight, "you are so brave."

She wiped her nose and sniffed back the tears. "I'll hold it for you. Get undressed."

Anna held the necklace as Ursula undressed. Then she put the necklace into Ursula's cupped hands. "Don't ever lose this, Ursula."

Ursula nodded, and Anna stood up just as a soldier stomped towards her.

"Hurry!" the Nazi hollered. His attention was drawn to Anna's feet. In the middle of the line of naked, barefooted women and children, he saw Anna was still wearing her shoes.

"Take off your shoes!"

More soldiers hurried into the building, bringing boxes and laying them on the metal table. Some soldiers were pushing wheelbarrows while other soldiers walked close, gathering the clothes and throwing them in. Something puzzled Anna. The soldiers didn't pick up the underwear; they left them lying on the floor.

"Sir, I am a cripple," Anna spoke shyly. "May I keep my corrective shoes?"

The Nazi looked down at her shoes. The sole of one shoe was two inches thicker than the other. He looked at her with repugnance.

"No," he said angrily. "Take off your shoes!"

Anna sighed and began to take off her shoes. She winced as she pulled off the left shoe. Her left foot was noticeably smaller than her right and bent awkwardly, her toes a mangled mass of flesh.

Ursula's mouth dropped open in shock. She had never seen her mother's deformity. Then she realized that she had never seen her mother without her shoes on.

Anna's shoes were deposited in the wheelbarrow.

The children stood in silence around their mother for a few moments. Hilda patted her mother's shoulder. "I'm sorry, Mumma," Hilda consoled her.

They then heard the sound of water spraying onto concrete.

"Get in the showers!" the Nazis shouted, pointing toward the right side opening in the concrete wall. The women turned and shuffled their way toward the opening, trying unsuccessfully to cover themselves with their arms. They tried to walk as one clustered mass, hoping to shield as much of their bodies as possible from the soldiers' glares. The soldiers, in turn, strode up and down the line, their eyes throbbing with noxious pleasure. They laughed, shouted disgusting remarks, and pointed. One soldier whistled at Hilda. She blushed and huddled closer to Mumma. Mumma put her arm around Hilda, glaring at the soldier. They turned their heads and kept walking. Walking without her corrective shoes was very difficult and painful, still Anna managed to keep apace with the others.

Inside the shower room was a long water pipe that ran atop the length of one wall. Every six inches, hot water squirted out of a hole. It was not enough water to provide adequate cleansing, but the people wandered through the steam and the scant streams of water to appease the Nazis who were watching. It wasn't slippery, but Hilda held on to Mumma to support her. Sophus took Hanrie's hand and helped him walk through. Ursula gripped the necklace tightly and stayed close behind Sophus. Together they exited on the other side of the shower room.

As they came through the doorway they passed a metal table. The open boxes on the table revealed many glass vials and syringes. Several men were filling syringes with the vials' contents. As each Jew passed, they were stopped. The man would pinch a section of skin and stab the needle into the arm, pushing the fluid inward. In front of Mumma and Hilda, a young girl about Ursula's age was receiving an injection.

"Ow," the young girl cried. The man administered the drug and pulled the needle out.

"Shut up, Jew!" he yelled, batting her across her head. She stumbled forward. Ursula watched wide-eyed. She was very afraid of needles and knew the Nazis would not show her any mercy either.

"Get in line!" the Nazis yelled as they paraded around the room.

Just a few more steps and Ursula would be standing in front of the man with the needle. Mumma and Hilda were already receiving their shots.

"Stay in line!" the Nazis commanded. Sophus and Hanrie were getting their needles and Hanrie was crying. Just one more step. "Hurry!" the Nazis screamed.

Mustn't scream, mustn't cry, Ursula kept repeating in her head. She held the necklace tightly in her hands as the man grabbed the skin of her arm. *Mustn't cry, mustn't scream.* He looked curiously at her hands as she held them tightly together. He shrugged his shoulders and plunged the needle deep into her arm. She held her breath, clenched her teeth and closed her eyes. *Mustn't, mustn't!* He withdrew the needle and she exhaled.

"Go on!" a soldier elbowed her forward.

More soldiers, more boxes. The Nazis reached into the boxes and handed each person a pile of clothing as they passed. Ursula held both her arms together as the man laid the small bundle across her arms.

"Hurry now, get your uniforms on!" the soldiers yelled.

They were directed to go back to the other side of the building where they had undressed. Anna investigated her pile of clothing; a blue and white striped smock, a gray sweater and wooden clogs. *No wonder they left the underwear on the floor,* she thought, *there's no underwear.* She looked at her children.

"We need to find our underwear," she said to them.

"No talking!" the Nazis commanded.

Anna lowered her head and led her children across the room. There they searched the floor for their undergarments.

"Hurry!" the soldiers shouted.

Finding their belongings, they set their uniforms on the bench. They scrambled to dress, but their skin was damp making it difficult to pull the clothing over their bodies. The uniforms were of cheaply made material, scratchy and uncomfortable. Ursula released the hidden necklace from her clenched fists, letting it drop gently onto the bench. Quickly she set her pile of clothing over it. As she dressed, she was careful to keep her back to the soldiers. She found that the smock had two lower pockets and one breast pocket. The breast pocket had a yellow patch of the Star of David sewn onto it. Inconspicuously, she slid the necklace into one of the lower pockets. As she put on her clogs, she saw Hanrie struggling with the buttons on his sweater.

"Let me help you, Hanrie," she said to him.

Hanrie held his stomach and cried.

"I know you're hungry, Hanrie. So am I."

She helped him button the sweater. As she looked at the others, she noticed that everyone had a gray sweater except her. She was just about to question her mother about this unfair oversight when the doors opened.

"Everybody out!" the Nazis directed.

They were steered out of the building and back into the holding area. The people in the yard scuffled about, looking for their families, almost unrecognizable now with their shaved heads and identical clothing. Anna saw Frederick and Ludwig.

"Fred!" Anna yelled. He turned toward her and smiled broadly. As they walked to each other Frederick saw that she was limping.

"Those savages wouldn't let you keep your shoes," his anger boiled.

"Don't talk so loud Fred. Please, I don't want anymore harm to come to you," she begged him, her voice cracking and her hands shaking as she touched his face. He wrapped his arms around Hanrie and Mumma.

Ludwig hugged Mumma too, but his attention was diverted by the voices he heard. Different languages floated in the air from the other side of the fence and he listened attentively trying to discern the conversations.

Hilda, Sophus and Ursula ran to Poppa. They held onto him so tight that it hurt him — but it was a good hurt. *Don't let me go, my angels,* he pleaded silently.

All at once the large gate opened and the grounds of Bergen-Belsen were made visible to them again. Gun-toting Nazis with barking canines then exploded into the yard.

The German Shepherds scared Little Hanrie and he clung to Mumma.

A commanding officer burst into the yard. "Attention," he bellowed, "adults are to go to that building over there on the far right and children over to the building on the left," he said while pointing.

Dozens of SS soldiers helped the commander fulfill his directives. They forcibly separated the people into groups, splitting the families. They pushed and shoved them into lines, calling them vile names, while their menacing dogs snapped at them. "Hurry, get in line!," they shouted.

One soldier wrenched Hanrie from Anna's arms and set him on the ground.

"No, no, my baby!" Anna screamed.

The soldier thrust Anna away. Frederick and Anna were forced into the formation that was moving out of the holding pen toward the right.

"Mum!" Hanrie objected. He sobbed and held his arms out for Mumma. A soldier kicked him aside. Ursula helped Hanrie to his feet and held on to his hand firmly. He jumped up and down urging Ursula to let him join Mumma.

"No, Hanrie, you must stay with me," Ursula entreated.

The soldiers steadily shoved and prodded the immense crowd of people out of the holding pen. The German Shepherds barked and growled.

"Get in line! Stay in line!"

The Swartz children were forced into the crowd moving to the left.

"Urshey, hold my hand!" Ludwig yelled to Ursula. She grabbed his hand and saw Hilda and Sophus beside him with their arms intertwined.

"Children, stay together!" Frederick yelled back, hoping that they could still hear him.

The Swartz children held onto each other, but with the hordes of soldiers pushing the crowd of people, Ursula felt her hold on Ludwig slipping. Then, helped by the prodding Nazis, her hand completely loosened from Ludwig's. Now Ursula was determined to hold on to Hanrie even more. She clamped both her hands onto his left hand, pulling him along.

Hanrie tried to push her hands off. "You will see Mumma later," she tried to reassure him, but he couldn't hear Ursula through his distressed cries for Mumma. He whined, pinching and pushing her hands. "Stop!"

Suddenly, Ursula was knocked to the ground by the pushing mob behind her, and Hanrie was freed. "No!" Ursula screamed as Little Hanrie ran toward Mumma.

Hilda, Ludwig and Sophus, in the midst of the mob, turned when they heard Ursula scream. They yelled for Hanrie to come back, but he didn't listen. The soldiers restrained them.

"Hanrie, stop! Hanrie, come back!" they shouted.

"Quiet! No talking!" the Nazis yelled at them. They watched helplessly as Hanrie ran toward Mumma and Poppa. A soldier's German Shepherd lunged at Hanrie.

Terrified, Hanrie screamed and jumped, but then started running again. Nothing was to stop him from reaching Mumma. The soldier holding the leash toyed with the dog, loosening then tightening his grip on the leash until he had driven his dog and the others into a fury.

Then the soldier let go of the leash.

Hanrie ran furiously, but the dog caught up to him and latched onto his leg. Hanrie screamed and fell to the ground. He tried to wiggle free, but the dog gripped even tighter.

"Mumma!" Hanrie cried in pain.

Another Nazi let go of his dog. It ran to Hanrie and it clamped its jaws tight around his other leg. Then another dog sprinted over and started chewing on Hanrie's arms. The soldiers were laughing.

"Oh, no, no, no!" Anna shrieked. Frederick and other Jews around them tried to restrain her.

"Oh God, my baby!" She wrestled with those who tried to hold her back. Though her physical condition had been weakened, as she watched her baby struggle against the gripping jaws of the dogs her strength intensified. She struggled relentlessly, smacking and kicking, and tore herself from the hold of Frederick and the others. She hobbled as quickly as she could toward Little Hanrie.

"Anna, please come back!" Frederick called. The others held onto Frederick urging him to stay in the line.

"My baby!" Anna wailed as she hobbled toward him.

The soldiers watched her. They laughed and pointed as she limped and cried hysterically.

"My baby, please!"

And when she was just a few feet from her precious destination, a soldier aimed his rifle and shot her.

Hanrie's little body jerked and Ursula could hear his stifled sobbing. Then the one soldier, the first to let his dog attack, walked over to little Hanrie. With a broad smile on his face he pulled out his gun, laid it directly on Hanrie's head and fired.

And then all the soldiers laughed.

Chapter Five

Ursula didn't realize how loud she was screaming. All she knew was the stabbing pain in her chest and the hard-ness of the ground. She lay there kicking her legs and pounding the earth with her fists. A soldier marched to her side, pointing his rifle.

"If you don't shut up the next bullet will be in your head!"

Horrified, Ludwig broke free from Hilda's grasp and ran to Ursula.

"Urshey, come on!" Ludwig implored.

Ludwig helped her to her feet. Her legs felt heavy and her eyes remained fixed on Mumma's and Hanrie's motion-less bodies.

"Urshey, we have to do what they say."

One dog was still attending to the body, nudging Hanrie with its nose, sniffing and licking. Ursula wailed hysterically as Ludwig led her to the building.

"Luddie, help!" Hilda cried, "He's taking Sophus!"

Ludwig looked as Sophus was being pried from Hilda's arms. Sophus struggled against the soldier who was pulling her along.

"Sophus!" Ludwig screamed.

He dropped Ursula's arm and started running toward Sophus. Another soldier stopped him.

"And just where do you think you're going?"

"My sister is being taken away!" Ludwig tried to go around him. "We have to stay together!"

Ursula and Hilda huddled together, watching their brother.

"No," the soldier commanded, "we say where you go! Now get back in line!"

He pointed to the line of children walking at gunpoint. There was a large fenced-in area that surrounded the building the line of children were being prodded toward. The gate was open and the children were being forced inside.

Ludwig looked at the soldier vacantly. He watched Sophus trying to free herself from the man's hold. *I have to get Sophus,* he thought. He tried again to walk around him.

"So, you don't listen, Jew," the soldier said as he pulled his arm back and let his fist fly into Ludwig's nose.

Hilda and Ursula heard the crack, like a light bulb bursting. Ludwig stumbled.

"Now get back in line!"

Defeated, Ludwig wearily joined the others. Hilda and Ursula clung to him. As the last of the new arrivals to Bergen-Belsen entered the yard, the gate was shut.

Hilda, Ursula and Ludwig sat down against the fence of the yard. Ludwig held his sweater to his nose. Tilting his chin upward, he tasted the blood dripping down his throat. Hilda held Ursula close to her, rocking gently as they both wept.

Inside the yard of the other building, Frederick leaned against the fence. He covered his face with his hands and sobbed. His body jerked in uncontrollable spasms as he mourned. *Oh, Anna why didn't you listen to me? Why didn't you ever listen to me?* He cursed her, and yet it was her strength and stubbornness that he had so loved. Other Jews approached him, laying their hands on his shoulders to console him, but in vain. He saw their lips and hands moving, but he could hear and feel nothing. He was numb. The evening sun stabbed his eyes and his stomach cramped. He thought he might regurgitate. It was then that someone new approached him.

A gypsy woman thrust her tarot cards in front of his face. "Want to know your future?"

The brightly colored pictures on the tarot cards shocked his senses, taking him aback. He almost laughed at the absurdity of her question. He shook his head no. She looked around cautiously.

"Want to save your children?" she asked him surreptitiously.

"What—yes—how?" he stammered.

"I know a man," she talked quickly. "He will get your children out of here."

She motioned for Frederick to follow her. They took a few steps and she pointed through the fence.

"See that man over there at the trucks?"

Frederick looked over. At the opposite end of the compound he saw a German soldier working on the military vehicles.

"The mechanic?" Frederick questioned.

"Yes. For a fee he will get your children out of here."

"For a fee!" Frederick exclaimed. "But I have nothing."

"You may have something that interests him," she looked at his watch.

My watch? He had been able to hide the watch from the guards as he undressed and showered. For a moment, he gazed at his watch. The sparkle reminded him of Anna's laughter, and he felt another sob bullying its way up his throat. *What if this woman is lying? But Anna would want me to do anything to save our children.*

"How many children?" the gypsy woman asked impatiently.

"Fi-," he stopped himself. He remembered Hanrie's cruel death. He lowered his eyes. "Four," he replied, for he had not seen Sophus being taken away.

"Four, that's a lot. I will talk to him," the gypsy woman said.

"Please do," petitioned Fred.

As Fred spoke, two Nazi guards appeared.

"Please do what?" they demanded, as they angrily pushed Frederick's shoulder.

"Please tell my future," Frederick thought quickly.

"I know your future and believe me you're better off not knowing it," the one soldier said. They both looked at each other and laughed. Then the other soldier acknowledged the gypsy woman.

"And you'd better stop causing an uproar around here with your stupid cards or you won't have a future," he said, while poking her in her chest and shoulder with his rifle.

"I'm sorry, sir," she said bowing her head.

"Did I ask you to speak, Gypsy?" He started to raise his hand to slap her but the other soldier stopped him.

"It's not worth it, let's go."

He lowered his hand and nodded in agreement. As they walked away he spat on her. The woman's head remained bowed.

"Sometimes I don't know what's worse, a Gypsy or a Jew," they heard the soldiers say as they walked away.

"I will make the arrangements," she said, wiping the spittle from her cheek. Speechless, Frederick watched her leave. Gratitude overwhelmed him.

May a thousand blessings be bestowed upon her, God!

Suddenly he felt light, intoxicated with hope. *I may die here, but my children will be free! My God, thank you, thank you, my God! My God, my God…*his silent prayer became audible praise. Nearby SS soldiers bustled around him, once again shouting at the Jews to form a line. A soldier overheard him.

"Shut up, you worthless pig! We're your god now!"

He pushed Frederick into a row of people and ordered them to start walking.

"Line up, mealtime!" The soldiers joked with each other.

"Some slop for the pigs!" the one SS who had pushed Frederick remarked.

"Do we really have to feed the pigs?" another soldier jokingly inquired.

"No, but we are generous!" one soldier answered.

They howled with laughter, and as they guided the Jews toward a building that housed one of the dining areas, they squealed like pigs.

"Line up, brats!" the Nazis called to the children in the yard.

Ursula had fallen asleep in Hilda's arms and was awakened by a warm puff of air. The SS walked by, their dogs so close that Ursula was stirred by their breath. The SS kicked at them.

"Get up! Get in line for your meal or you get nothing!" they yelled.

The children dashed into place not wanting to miss the only meal of the day. Ursula was surprised by the number of children who poured out of the building that contained the bunks. She reasoned by their gaunt figures and apathetic expressions that they had been at Bergen-Belsen for a long time. Ursula walked along with them. Glancing back, she noticed that some people stayed behind, too weak to move. *Aren't they going to eat?* she wondered. Her stomach growled and her attention turned to the moving line that she was swept into.

Hilda, Ludwig and Ursula followed the others. They passed through the open gate and were led through the compound. Curiously they gazed at their surroundings. Mumma's and Hanrie's bodies still lay on the ground. They clutched each other. Dotted all over the compound were piles of bodies, many clothed, but some not. The Shepherd dogs snarled at the children.

"Hurry, hurry!" Fearfully they obeyed.

There were hundreds of Jews moving in organized lines. The SS strode alongside, berating and intimidating them with their rifles and fierce dogs. "Stay in line! Hurry!"

Ursula and Ludwig scanned the formations looking for Sophus and Poppa.

"Luddie, do you see Poppa and Sophus?" Ursula whispered.

"Not yet," he replied.

"Quiet! No talking!" the Nazis scolded.

The children were led into a building which housed a dining hall. They were handed a small melamine plate, a cup and a piece of twine as they entered. The twine puzzled Ursula, but then she saw those who had been at the camp longer, untying the strings from around their waists, freeing their cups and plates. The line moved quickly. As they passed a big pot, the soldier behind it ladled a portion onto each plate. The soldier standing beside him then laid a piece of bread on the plate. The next big pot was full of water. All the Jewish children walked by, dipping their cups in it. Then they moved over to the dining table.

There were several long dining tables. Benches of comparable length ran along each side. The Swartz children sat together at one. Looking at their tablemates, they were disgusted by the undignified manner with which the others ate. Given no utensils, they watched as everyone had to eat with their hands. And when the plates were empty of food, they licked them for every last morsel. The children realized this is how they must now eat, too. So they ate.

Mumma would scold me for this, Ursula thought. As they continued their meal, the Nazis walked close, chuckling and nodding their heads, pleased with how they forced the Jews to debase themselves.

"Get up!" the SS yelled. "Get out!"

Dinnertime was over.

Hilda, Ludwig and Ursula watched the others tie the plates and cups to their waists with the twine.

"If you lose your plate, you get no food," said a young girl of Ursula's age. She sat across the table staring at the Swartz children, her eyes the color of a robin's egg surrounded by long black lashes. Her mouth twitched slightly as she showed Ursula how to tie the cup and plate around her waist. They smiled at each other.

"No talking!" the Nazis commanded. "Time to leave!"

The children scrambled over the benches, back into the organized line that led them out of the dining hall, across the compound and back into the yard that encompassed the sleeping bunkers.

The gate shut behind them, but the despair beyond the gate could not be shut out. Ursula slumped to the ground next to the fence listening to the screaming, the sobbing and the occasional gunfire. Ludwig stooped down by her side.

"Now, Urshey, listen to me," Ludwig placed his hand on her shoulder. "Don't talk. Don't look the Germans in the eyes. Keep your head down. If they talk to you, just nod your head. Let them think you're dumb."

"Okay," she agreed.

"No," he covered her mouth with his hand, "not one word."

She trembled slightly, feeling the urgency of his words. She nodded her head yes.

"I will watch over you. We must be careful. Now, I'm going to see what I can find out. Stay right here where I can find you."

As she watched him walk away, she leaned her head back on the fence, giving the slowly evading evening sun her whole countenance.

She saw Ludwig talking to a woman. The woman held cards in her hand.

Cards, that's strange, thought Ursula. *The Germans let her have some cards.* She thought about the necklace in her pocket. *Or maybe they don't know she has them.* She slid her hand over her pocket to make sure the necklace was still there. She sighed with relief and closed her eyes, eventually nodding off.

"Little girl, wake up," urged the woman, shaking Ursula lightly.

No, I wasn't sleeping, couldn't have been sleeping.

Ursula looked up at the sinking sun's changed position. The gypsy woman smiled and held out her cards. "I'm going to tell you your future."

She sat on the ground and spread the cards out in front of her. Two German soldiers stood nearby, watching them. "This card means happiness," she said, pointing to one of the cards. The Gypsy watched from the corner of her eye as the German soldiers started moving toward her and Ursula. "Oh, but this one means trouble," she said. The soldiers came closer, sneering at the woman. "And this one means good luck." She bowed her head and waited for them to pass. "I do not have much longer to live," she said, after the soldiers were assuredly out of earshot. "But, don't you worry little girl," she gazed at Ursula, "you are

"The gypsy woman smiled and held out her cards. 'I'm going to tell you your future.' She sat on the ground and spread the cards out in front of her."

going to live a long life." She touched her cards, pretending to be reading them. "I know your brother, Ludwig. He will take care of you. You are leaving this place. See those bushes over there?"

There were three small clumps of bushes in front of the fence. Ursula nodded her head yes.

"Tomorrow night, as soon as it gets dark, you hide behind those bushes. A man will stop his truck next to the gate. When he blinks the lights twice, you run to the truck and get in. You hide quietly and you run quickly, do you understand?"

Ursula nodded yes.

The gypsy woman gathered her cards and stood up. "You will be okay. Ludwig is a smart boy. And always remember, your father loves you very much."

The gypsy woman turned and walked away.

I am leaving this place! Ursula felt excitement, joy and fear. *Why did she tell me to remember my father loves me, isn't he going, too?*

Some German soldiers walked close by. Ursula remembered her brother's words and lowered her head. They walked away and Ursula looked up. Her brother was walking toward her, nodding his head in approval. He held his hand out and helped her up. He wrapped his arm protectively around her shoulders and took her over to the building. They went in and found an empty bunk where they both lay down. Hilda came in a few moments later and settled into another empty bunk.

"Good night, Urshey," both Hilda and Ludwig said.

She lay there quietly, her thoughts spinning wildly. She repeated the Gypsy's words to herself, going over tomorrow's planned escape again and again. *Sleep? How can I sleep?* She listened to the mournful sounds surrounding her — the sobbing, the barking dogs, the shouting soldiers. *Sleep? How... can...I...*

Chapter Six

Before Ursula fully awakened she sensed someone's gaze upon her. She opened her eyes. Across the slim aisle, in another bunk, the girl with the blue, robin's egg colored eyes was staring at her. The girl's mouth twitched while she moved her fingers in a wave-like manner.

"I'm Lise," she stated.

Ursula was slightly irritated by her. *That's not what I'll call you*, she thought. *I shall call you Little Miss Robin Egg.* Ursula smiled at the thought of it.

"They killed my parents. They shot them right in front of me," Lise said.

The statements slapped Ursula like a hand across her mouth. She buried her face in her hands. *Shut up, Little Miss Robin Egg! I don't want to remember anything of yesterday, only the gypsy woman's words!*

"They like to make you watch," Lise said coldly.

If you don't shut up I will have to hit you! Ursula silently screamed.

The doors to the bunker building burst open and some Nazi soldiers strutted inside. One of them held a clipboard and began reading the names on it.

"If your name is read, line up at the door," one of the SS men commanded.

Hilda, Ludwig and Ursula's names were on the list. Confused and upset, they looked at each other.

What? Did we do something wrong? Ursula wondered. She glanced at Lise.

"You're getting another needle," Lise said.

Ludwig helped Ursula to her feet.

Oh, no! Not another needle! Maybe Little Miss Robin Egg is wrong.

Ludwig placed his arm around Ursula's shoulder and they lined up at the door. Just outside the door, sitting at a metal table, were several men filling syringes. Once again the Jews were forced to walk in front of the table and, as they passed, they received an inoculation. After that, they were allowed to walk around inside the yard.

Ursula held her hand over the injection site. *No more needles, we are leaving tonight,* she thought.

Ursula decided to investigate the yard, especially the bushes.

"Urshey, you can look around, just stay where I can see you," Ludwig told her.

She surveyed the area. It was a barren, rectangular yard and there was not a section where Ursula would be out of Ludwig's view. Still, she knew her brother's good intentions, so she walked carefully and slowly. She saw Hilda smiling and talking to one of the young Nazi guards, his hand patting her shoulder.

Ursula stood next to the bushes that the gypsy woman had pointed to. Looking around cautiously, making sure that none of the roaming SS soldiers were paying any attention to her, she peered behind the bushes to see how much space was available. She smiled. *Plenty of room for all of us. Luddie, Sophus, Hilda and me. Wait…Sophus! Where is Sophus? We can't leave without Sophus!* Ursula panicked. She looked wildly from side to side. No hands were around her throat, yet she felt like she was suffocating. She gasped for air and ran to the other side of the yard. Here she could see into most of the compound, but some areas were hidden from her view brcause of the surrounding buildings. *Must …find…Sophus!* She crept her way along the fence, looking for Sophus. She searched frantically, all the while gasping for air.

Two nearby SS soldiers watched her. "She's gone mad," the one said.

"Looks like it," the other one replied. "They all do eventually. We'll keep an eye on her. If she gets violent, we can shoot her." The soldiers nodded in agreement.

Ursula searched fiendishly, concentrating on seeing around the buildings. Finally she reached a place where she thought she could see almost all of Bergen-Belsen. Her excitement rose. She studied the compound beyond her reach, searching for Sophus. What she saw frightened and nauseated her.

All around her Jews lumbered by. Their skin and uniforms were covered with filth making them look

monochrome gray. Their gray skin clung to their pro-
truding bones as they plodded along silently, with glaring,
ghostly, catatonic eyes.

Ursula listened to their moaning and labored breathing.
She noticed their hands. Every bone of their fingers was
visible, like no layer of tissue surrounded them. *They're not
people, they're skeletons.* They had become walking skeletons
in the sepulcher of Belsen. She was sickened by the Nazis'
cruelty. They beat the skeletons with their rifle butts and
they let their dogs jump on them and bite them. She wanted
to cry out, "Leave them alone," but she dared not.

Farther to the right, she watched the Germans pour a
liquid onto a mound of dead bodies and set it on fire. She
strained to see if Mumma's and Hanrie's bodies were still
lying on the ground, but she could not see over far enough.
Then she looked at the ground in front of her. Two dead
bodies lay a few feet from the fence. Judging by the shapes
of the bodies, Ursula assumed it to be a man and a woman.
But as Ursula stared at the bodies, she noticed something
more. It appeared to her that there was a third body. It lay
cradled under the two and all Ursula could see was what
she thought to be a small part of a face.

Is that really another person underneath?

She strained to move closer and unintentionally kicked
some dust and pebbles onto the bodies. Suddenly the eye
of the small, hidden face opened, staring directly at Ursula.
She gasped and fell backwards onto her bottom. Nearby
SS who had been watching her, broke out in laughter.
Ludwig ran to Ursula's side.

"Urshey, are you all right?" he asked while assisting
her to her feet. He leaned close to her ear. "Don't attract
their attention, Urshey," he scolded her.

She looked at him in disbelief. Surely he didn't think she meant to fall! Surely he had known the importance of what she was trying to accomplish, to find Sophus! Her mouth dropped open as he looked at her sternly, yet she yielded to her brother and followed him to the bunker building.

Petr trembled with fear when the pebble hit his face. Thinking the Germans were close, he opened his eye, just the one eye because the other was flat against the hard ground. He saw the child looking at him, and the look of shock and surprise that she displayed.

Please, God, he prayed fearfully, *please don't let them find me.* He almost began crying again. *I shouldn't have looked.* But he did look, and now Petr was worried that the soldiers would move him and his parents' bodies and discover that he was still alive.

Yesterday the Nazis had shot him and his parents from behind. He had not felt a bullet penetrate his own flesh, but his parents' bodies slumped over and knocked him to the ground, covering him. Even with their final breaths, they were protecting him. When the Germans came over to examine the bodies, Petr stayed silent and still. It worked. They thought Petr was dead, too. Petr didn't understand why the Germans would sometimes let the dead remain where they fell for days, even weeks — and other times dispose of them quickly. How long would they let him and his dead parents lay undisturbed? He hoped it would be long enough to allow for his escape.

Petr saw the truck last night. The headlights flicked twice, then a man got out and went to the back of the truck. He then watched as children ran to the truck and jumped inside. He saw the man working at the back of the truck. Then he watched the truck drive away. Petr swore that if he ever saw the truck again he would wriggle out from beneath his parents' bodies, run over to the truck and get in. His hope of freedom could be a reality as long as the man came back with the truck, and as long as the Germans didn't move him and his parents' dead bodies.

Petr became angered. *But that cursed child almost gave my hiding place away! I shouldn't have opened my eye! I should've waited for the night! Oh, please God, let the truck come back. And please, don't let them move us,* he prayed.

He lay still, trying to hold back his tears, waiting for the sun to set.

On the other side of the compound, near the garage, the gypsy woman walked quickly. She was dangerously close to the restricted area. If she was caught, the punishment would be severe. But that's where she had to go to make the exchange; one gold watch for four children. "Lovely trinket," he had said.

Trinkets, the gypsy woman thought. Every payment that she had brought to the mechanic, he called a trinket. She shook her head. Didn't he realize the worth beyond monetary of the precious mementos that she was bringing him? Heirloom jewelry, wedding and engagement rings, gifts from loved ones—pieces of people's lives. Without hesitation, they gave all they had left. They gave anything for their everything - the children. She hoped that she could go on making these exchanges until the end—the end of the war, or the end of her life.

She heard twigs snapping and shuffling stones behind her.

"Halt!"

She froze, her body tingling with fear. She waited for him to catch up to her. The young German soldier stood in front of her. *Good, he's alone,* she thought. *I may be able to bargain my way out of this.*

Then she heard more footsteps behind her. Another soldier came and stood in front of her. She swallowed hard.

"Why are you near the restricted area? See the sign." He pointed to the sign with red letters that said, "No Trespassing."

"Maybe she can't read. She's just a gypsy," the other soldier replied.

"Oh, but she can read the future," he chuckled to his partner. "You have been told to stop causing a ruckus with your stupid cards. Where are your cards?"

She slowly moved her hand and pointed to her pocket.

"Well, come on, bring them out."

She sensed anger and ridicule in his voice. Producing the cards quickly, the sneering solder grabbed them from her hands and picked one from the stack.

"Look, this one means love," he said holding it up. He handed it to his comrade who tore it in half and threw it on the ground. The gypsy woman gasped and watched in horror.

"This one stands for money." He gave the card to the other soldier, and again he tore it and threw it on the ground. The German chortled as he held up another. "And this one definitely means death."

He threw all of the tarot cards onto the ground. They both laughed. And as they watched her scramble to pick up her cards, they pulled out their guns and shot her.

Dinnertime, and Ursula was glad. She had lain in the bunk for hours wondering what was louder—the moaning, the sobbing, or her growling stomach. Her cup and plate were tied securely to her waist, just like the others. She advanced into the line with Hilda and Ludwig as the Nazis commanded. "Hurry!" they yelled.

Ursula noticed Lise behind her. Lise smiled at Ursula, a quick twitch of her mouth. Ursula smiled back and then she wondered, was Lise really smiling at her or was it just a nervous habit?

The line moved quickly and once again Ursula saw those too weak to move forgoing another meal. As the line moved through the compound to the dining hall, the Swartz children saw that Mumma's and Hanrie's dead bodies had not been taken away.

"Stay in line! Hurry!" the Nazis shouted.

Ursula looked for Poppa and Sophus. They kept silent, but Ursula could tell by the way Hilda's and Luddie's heads were bobbing about that they too were searching. Then they saw Poppa!

In another line, Frederick walked along with others at gunpoint. Frederick was going in the opposite direction, but it seemed as though the lines would pass each other. Ludwig grabbed Ursula's hand.

The line of Jews in which Poppa marched was getting closer and closer. Excitement pulsated through their hands like an electrical charge. Closer, closer. They waved at Poppa. Tears filled Luddie's eyes, for he knew that this may be the last chance to ever see Poppa again. Poppa was crying too, but his eyes were not filled with sadness, only hope and love.

My children, be brave, your time here is almost over. God, protect them, give them strength, give them wisdom, he prayed.

Cautiously, with his arm still straight and elbow to his side, he lifted his hand and waved quickly. There was something different about Poppa's hand. Though his hand had been raised for only a second, Ursula sensed that something had changed.

"No talking!" the Germans shouted. Their Nazi-controlled greetings ended. The line containing the Swartz children and the line with Frederick were taken into two different dining halls.

Inside the building, the children untied the plates and cups from their waists. Ursula noticed the word Belsen engraved on the underside of the plate. They obtained their food and drinks as before and sat down. Downcast, Ludwig picked at his meal.

Lise sat across the table watching him. "It's the only food you get; you should eat it," she said to him.

He looked up at her and tears rolled down his face, dropping onto the plate. He was missing Poppa already.

"They killed my parents," Lise said, looking directly at him. Her long, black lashes were motionless. She took a bite of food. "They like to make you watch."

Ludwig sighed, and ate the food mingled with his tears.

Finished with the meal, they were led back into the yard that encompassed the bunker building. Ludwig and

Hilda walked together, talking intently. Ursula sat down with her back against the fence, straight across from the bushes. She went over the escape plan again and again. Ursula glanced over at Ludwig. He seemed to be quarreling with Hilda.

"You'll get what's coming to you!" Ludwig yelled back at Hilda as he walked away from her. He shook his head as he sat down next to Ursula.

"Ursula," he said, as he patted her leg, "always remember what Mumma said. 'Do good to others and good things will happen to you, but if you treat others badly, bad things will happen to you.'"

She nodded her head yes, and then gave him a puzzled look. He leaned down and whispered in her ear, "Hilda's not coming with us." Her eyes widened. "She's afraid to leave. And besides that," he pointed to Hilda, "the Germans gave her a job."

Ursula looked over and saw Hilda with a long, thin stick in her hand chasing and beating some children around her. Ludwig leaned his shoulders and head back against the fence. "She gets to take care of the children."

They sat in silence, waiting for the sun's descent.

Nightfall crept in and Ludwig took Ursula's hand. "We'll walk around the yard slowly," he whispered, "and as soon as we see that no one is watching us, we'll hide behind the bushes."

Standing up, they strolled the yard, hand in hand, until they neared the bushes. All the while Ludwig inconspicuously watched the soldiers. As soon as the soldiers turned their backs, Ludwig and Ursula slipped behind the bushes. To their amazement, they weren't alone.

A small heap sat curled on the ground between the dense clump of bushes and the fence. Ludwig and Ursula had startled it. They heard a gasp. Ludwig bent down. "Shh," he whispered, "What are you doing here?"

"The gypsy woman said," the small heap whispered back.

Ludwig patted the child's shoulder in acknowledgement and wondered how they were to get out of the yard from behind the bushes. Kneeling down, he noticed the bottom of the fence was weak and slightly pushed out. He began digging at the dirt with his hands, creating more space for their escape. Excitedly, Ursula and the other child began to help Ludwig dig. When Ludwig was satisfied that the hole was deep enough, he nodded his head and gestured for them to stop. He held Ursula's hand and they sat next to the other child, hiding together behind the bushes, anticipating the headlights.

The yard surrounding the bunker building was quiet, but in the distance they could hear the sounds of wickedness: wailing and screaming people, gunshots, barking dogs and the shouting and laughing of the SS. The evil felt like thick, black tar enshrouding them. They could see nothing in front of them, yet Mumma's and Hanrie's still bodies flashed in Ursula's mind. Then, suddenly, amidst the horrific clamor, they heard an approaching vehicle stop.

Ludwig squeezed Ursula's hand. They saw the automobile's headlights. They heard the door opening and someone's footsteps. Ludwig felt his heart pounding in his chest. Then the headlights blinked twice! The signal! Ludwig pushed the fence as far as he could and Ursula and the other child darted out from underneath. Ludwig squirmed out from under the fence and he and the other two children ran toward the lights. As they were running, Ludwig noticed more children coming out from behind other bushes. *Oh God, please don't let us get caught!*, he thought.

Petr saw the truck. In elation, he scrambled out from beneath his parents' bodies and ran to the truck. *Oh God, please don't let us get caught*, Petr prayed.

The man stood at the back of the truck, and as he saw the approaching children he waved for them to get in the back. He held his finger up against his lips, urging the children to be quiet. Sweat dripped down his back and the hair on his arms pricked outward. *Hurry, dear children, hurry!* Morbidly clear of his consequences, he implored, *Oh God, please don't let us get caught!*

All of the children quickly jumped into the back of the truck and lay down on the floor. The man took the false bottom that he had constructed and slid it back into place, completely covering the children. Then he got into the driver's seat and started to drive away. He let out a deep breath, yet he knew there was more danger to overcome: the checkpoint.

Two armed guards stood at the gate. The mechanic stopped his vehicle and one of the guards stepped over to the open driver's side window. The man smiled and nodded to the guard, covering his mouth as he yawned.

"Hello Karl," the guard said, "Ready for bed, huh?"

"Oh, I am worked like a dog," he replied. In the side mirrors he could see the other guard inspecting the sides and back of the truck. He became uneasy and yawned again, rubbing his temples with his fingers. The guard smiled.

"Hurry up back there," he called to the other guard, "Karl needs to go home."

"It's clean," he said walking up to his comrade's side. "We are all overworked," the guard commented, patting Karl's shoulder. "Drive safely."

The guards opened the gate and Karl drove the truck through the checkpoint.

"Goodnight, Karl!" they called out in unison.

Karl politely waved as he passed. He wiped the sweat from his brow, grateful that the hidden children had remained quiet, and headed eastward to the Naturpark.

Chapter Seven

Ludwig held tightly to Ursula's hand as the children rode in total darkness. At first the route seemed fairly smooth, but the longer they rode the bumpier the travel became. They dared not utter a sound, even when the bumps in the road caused their bodies to bounce and their heads to hit the wooden floor above them.

Karl drove as deep into the forest as the thickening grove of trees would allow. He would drop these children off in a different location from the previous ones.

At last he came to a suitable place and stopped the truck. Before him was a large thicket, and beyond that the dense, black forest. Some trees had fallen, making it impassable by vehicle. He got out of the truck and walked to the back. His pulse quickened as he looked around.

No houses, good.

A full moon shone brightly through the trees in the evening sky with no clouds to encumber its glow.

This is good, Karl thought, *they'll have enough light.*

He scanned the road behind him to be sure he was alone. He worked hurriedly, sliding out the truck's false bottom and setting it on the ground.

"You can come out now," he said.

Karl ran back to the opened door of the truck. He reached behind the driver's seat and retrieved a large, brown bag and a gallon jug full of water, then returned to the children.

The children, stiff and sore from the ride, fumbled out of the truck. Petr was the first one out. Stepping aside, he smiled and inhaled deeply. Next, Lise exited the truck, followed by the rest of the children, with Ludwig and Ursula being last. Ursula patted her pocket, assuring the prism necklace's safety.

As Ludwig and Ursula stretched, something shiny in the truck caught Ursula's attention. She stepped toward it. The glint came from gold colored buttons on a soldier's coat. It was indiscriminately folded on an interior seat in the back of the truck. *Someone must have forgotten their coat,* Ursula thought.

Karl motioned for the children to gather around him. Ursula grabbed the coat and followed the others.

"Take this," Karl said. He handed each child a circular loaf of bread. "Eat it slowly; it may be all you have for a while." He had one loaf too many.

"Wait," he shook his head, "I thought there was to be seven of you." He sighed. He shuddered to think of why the other child was absent. "Here, take it easy on this too," he said, giving the gallon jug of water and the extra loaf to the tallest boy. He singled out Ludwig and pulled him aside. "You take this." He handed Ludwig a flashlight. "Find your way in the forest. This is the Naturpark east of Belsen. You're a smart boy. I know you and the others will find a way to live. If you see anyone, don't tell anybody about me. I will try to get other children out, but it will be hard now, now that they have killed the gypsy woman."

Ludwig stared in disbelief. He thought fondly of the woman who had helped them to escape and he suddenly felt nauseated.

"I promise, I won't tell anyone about you," Ludwig said.

"Good boy," Karl said, patting his shoulder.

They turned, and Karl walked with the children to the beginning of the thicket.

"I will stay here and keep the headlights shining for you. When I can no longer see you, I will leave. Remember, help each other."

The children nodded their heads.

"Yes, sir. Thank you, sir," Ludwig said.

While the rest of the children echoed their gratitude, Lise grabbed his hand and kissed it. Tears welled in Karl's eyes.

"Hurry, now," he pointed to the woods. "Good luck, children."

They started their trek through the woods. He waved and the children waved in return.

Ursula saw an object on Karl's wrist sparkle with the moonlight. She was struck by the familiarity and stood still for a moment. *I've seen that before.*

"Come on, Urshey," Ludwig prompted.

"While the rest of the children echoed their gratitude, Lise grabbed his hand and kissed it."

She shook her head and stepped briskly to catch up with the rest of the children. By the truck's headlights, they were able to see each other. Ursula noticed there were two other girls. Lise was one of them, but she hadn't seen the other girl before in the camp. She looked to be a little older than Ursula. She had a sharp chin that protruded outward. Ursula thought it looked awkward compared to her other pretty, feminine features.

The girl saw Ursula looking at her. "I'm Nikki."

"I'm Ursula," she responded.

Counting Ludwig, there were three boys. One boy was much taller than Ludwig; he had a pleasant face that seemed to be smiling even when he wasn't. Ursula guessed the other boy to be around her age, and upon hearing their introductions, he added, "My name is Petr."

Petr looked strangely odd to Ursula. His body seemed disproportionately small compared to his head. He had a large square face with big, bulging eyes. He concentrated on eating his bread as he walked, which made him clumsy. Ursula imagined that the weight of his head might make him fall forward.

Then Lise, wanting to be included in the conversations, spoke also. "My name is Lise."

The headlights were becoming dimmer. The children crested a small hill and the lights vanished.

"He's gone," Lise said. "We're alone."

Suddenly Ursula remembered the gleam on the driver's wrist...could it be?

"Luddie, I think he was wearing Poppa's watch," Ursula remarked.

"Maybe it was, maybe it wasn't," Ludwig answered.

"I know it was," Ursula stated.

"Look," the tallest boy spoke, "I don't want to be mean, but we might *not* be alone. There could be Germans hiding behind the trees. They could be all around us. I think we need to be quiet until morning."

They took a few steps in silence, comprehending his warning.

"Okay, you may be right," said Nikki. "So I think we should just find a place to sleep and continue walking tomorrow in the daylight."

"Yes, good idea," Ludwig replied.

They kept walking until Ludwig's flashlight shone upon a clearing. "This looks like a good place."

They all agreed and sat down in a circle. Ludwig set the flashlight down in the middle of their circle.

"We might as well eat our bread now, the ants will have it by morning," Ludwig said. "Let's say grace."

They ate their loaves. The tallest boy set the jug of water next to the flashlight and then divided the extra loaf among them all. Since they still had their plates and cups tied around their waists, they untied the cups to fill with water.

Ursula noted Ludwig's face. His sorrowful expression stirred her.

"Luddie, is there something troubling you?"

Ludwig glanced at Ursula. In the faint peripheral light from the flashlight, he could see deeply into her eyes — his feisty, red-headed comrade of a kindred spirit. No, he could never keep a secret from her.

"The gypsy woman is dead. They killed her," he solemnly dropped his head.

"The woman who helped us escape?" Nikki and Ursula asked.

"Yes."

"Oh, no! They are wicked," Nikki lashed out.

The girls started to cry.

"Shh," the tallest boy reminded them.

"Shouldn't we say a prayer for her?" Lise whispered while sniffling.

"You can if you want," Ludwig answered. "She's in a better place now. She's free from Belsen."

"I'll say a word for her," the tallest boy began, and in a low voice, "God, thank you for the gypsy woman. Take care of her family. She helped to free us from Belsen."

The children eyed him as he lifted his cup in the air. "From this day forward, we are forever grateful to gypsies."

Following his example, the others held their cups up high.

"Forever grateful to gypsies," the children echoed. They sobbed quietly as they ate.

"The man who helped us escape," began Ludwig in a soft voice, "said that we are to help each other." He looked around the circle, then pointed to the tallest boy and himself. "We are the oldest, so we will be in charge. Is that agreeable to everyone?"

All the children nodded their heads.

"Good. Now we'll go around the circle this way and everyone will tell their name." He pointed to Ursula who was beside him, and one by one, they stated their name.

"Ursula."

"Lise."

"Petr."

"Nikki."

"Kurt."

"And I'm Luddie. We must agree to stay together, to look out for each other, and if need be, to fight for each other. Okay, let's sleep now. We'll travel more tomorrow," Ludwig suggested.

The children took off their gray sweaters and rolled them into a ball for a pillow. Ursula used her newfound possession, the soldier's coat, as her pillow. All but Ludwig and the tallest boy bedded down on the grass and twigs.

"So your name is Luddie?" the oldest boy asked.

"Ludwig, but people call me Luddie. You are Kurt, right?"

"Yes." They exchanged handshakes.

"How old are you, Kurt?"

"Sixteen, and you?"

"Twelve."

"I'll take first watch," Kurt volunteered. "When I feel myself falling asleep, I'll wake you."

"Okay."

Ludwig lay down.

Karl had mixed emotions as he drove home. He knew he would certainly be put to death if caught, and yet the tremendous joy he felt as he waved goodbye to the children was too addictive to stop. He felt like a king — King Karl, children's savior! And it all started with a promise of love.

He and his wife, Adele, had longed for a large family, but after several miscarriages they resigned themselves to the reality that they may be childless. Karl accepted it and was content to live the rest of his life with his beautiful Adele, but Adele was deeply saddened. They were contemplating adoption, when Adele was diagnosed with an incurable disease. Coinciding with the time of her diagnosis, the Nazi regime overpowered their town, taking all the Jews as prisoners. And while Adele did not object to the concentration camp near their home, or the taking away of the offensive Jews, what she did mind was the frightened faces of the children.

"They are innocent children," she said to Karl, "they don't deserve such cruelty." As she lay in pain, she made her dying request. "Karl, do whatever you can to save as many children as possible. Promise me." He loved her, so he promised her what he thought was impossible. She died with the harsh winter wind blowing outside.

Karl became quiet and reserved; friends and neighbors assumed he was in mourning. What they didn't know was how every night he sat at his lonely table trying to think of ways to accomplish the task his wife had bidden him. What could he do as a lowly mechanic in the nearby concentration camp? Then the idea occurred to him and the secret construction of the false bottom began. When he met the gypsy woman and confided in her about his plan, the die was cast.

He spoke to a picture taped to the dashboard.

"But now the gypsy woman is gone. Who will help me now? Maybe they suspect me of treason; maybe they will kill me, too. What do I do now, Adele?"

He looked at her picture and smiled.

"Yes, I know exactly what you would tell me: 'There

are so many more children to save!'" He shook his head. "Well, I have to find someone to help me."

He admired the watch on his wrist—Poppa's watch.

"I've never had such a fine watch; I'd like to keep this trinket," he sighed, "but I know what you would say: 'We need the money for flashlights and bread and gas.'"

He sighed again, louder than before. "I need someone to help me." *God, give me someone who will help me,* he prayed as he drove the rest of the way home.

Chapter Eight

Ursula awakened to the scent of moss. She saw that Ludwig was already awake, laying on his side with his head propped up on his arm. The flashlight was off and on the ground in front of him. He smiled at her. "Have you been awake all night, Luddie?" she asked.

The rest of the children were beginning to stir.

"Oh, yes," he teased her, "and in the middle of the night a bear came and I wrestled him and scared him away, saving us all."

She sat up smiling. "Stop, Luddie."

Everyone was waking, stretching and yawning.

"I'm hungry," Kurt yawned. He was a tall, lanky boy with an insatiable appetite.

"I wonder what day it is," inquired Nikki, rubbing her eyes.

"It is the day of our freedom," Kurt declared.

They were silent, letting their minds ingest his declaration. They looked at each other and smiles erupted across their dirty faces. Petr was rocking back and forth giggling.

Ursula thought of the crystal prism. *Maybe this will be our smooth, good day.*

"But, what do we do now? Where do we go?" Nikki asked.

"I want to go home!" interjected Lise.

"Yes, me too," agreed Nikki.

Petr and Ursula resonated.

"We can't go home! We don't have homes! The Germans took our homes, remember!" Kurt yelled indignantly.

Saddened, the children hushed. Ludwig pitied their sullen faces.

"It's true, we can't go home now. We can go home after the war, but now we must get out of Germany," Ludwig stated. Remembering maps of Germany that he had seen in his text books, and where the mechanic had disposed them, he continued, "We need to go west toward Holland; it's the shortest way out of Germany. I was watching the sun rise this morning, and it came up from over there, so we need to go in the opposite direction."

He pointed and Kurt nodded. "The mechanic told me that we are east of Bergen-Belsen, so first we'll have to travel south for a while so that when we turn west we won't end up back at Belsen."

The children's eyes widened.

"I'm afraid," said Lise.

"Don't worry, we'll stay together. No one must ever be alone," Kurt emphasized, his eyes sweeping wildly to each face. "We'll watch each other. And remember, Ludwig fought a bear in the wee hours of the morning."

Lise smiled and Nikki chuckled while Ludwig blushed.

"So come on, troops, let's go," Kurt said, jumping to his feet.

They all rose, picking up their belongings, making sure their cups and plates were tied securely. It was warm, so they tied their sweaters around their waists. Ludwig picked up the flashlight and Kurt carried the gallon jug. They started walking.

"Wait a minute," Kurt stopped them. With a scowl, he looked down at the yellow star on his breast pocket. "We won't let them win," he proclaimed as he tore it off and threw it down.

In agreement, they all tore off the stars from their uniforms and threw them to the ground. But Ludwig gazed at the star in his hand for a moment, the Star of David, the Hebrew symbol of strength, unity and victory. The Nazis had taken their sign of faith and corrupted it into a placard of debasement and oppression. *One day I will be able to wear this with honor.* Disheartened, Ludwig tilted his hand and the star glided gently to the ground. "Okay, let's go this way," Ludwig motioned for them to follow him.

They walked with trepidation.

"Watch the birds in the trees," Kurt said, "if they startle it may mean Germans are near."

They gazed at the trees as they walked.

"Stop!" Something had attracted Ludwig's attention. "Shh, listen."

They stood still and listened. It was the sound of gurgling water.

"That is a stream and we need to follow it," Luddie pointed in the direction of the gurgling sound, "because houses are built along waterways."

They walked hurriedly to the stream.

"Why do we need to find houses?" Ursula asked in surprise.

"We can't stay in these uniforms," Luddie answered.

Kurt nodded in agreement. "Also, we need to find food," he added, as rabbits and squirrels skittered across their path.

"There's food right at our feet," Petr said, pointing to the small animals darting in front of them.

"I won't eat little bunny rabbits," Lise complained.

"Yes, Petr," Kurt replied, ignoring Lise's remark, "and I brought extra twine from the camp." He pointed to his waist. "I can fashion a trap."

Ludwig grinned at Kurt and Petr's excited faces.

"True, fellows," Ludwig interrupted, "but how will we cut it up and cook it? Let's keep walking. Look out for people."

They continued walking parallel to the stream, all the while searching the sky, watching the birds and listening for airplanes. They walked for hours, following the stream, until finally the trees started to thin out.

"Look," Kurt pointed. The stream turned to the left, but in front of them was a dirt road.

"We must leave the forest with caution," Luddie warned them. Slowly, they stepped onto the side of the road and stopped. A short distance away they saw a cluster of homes.

The homes were visibly damaged by bombs and artillery fire.

"The SS has already been here," Kurt said. "I wonder if they're still here."

They watched for people, automobiles, animals — anything that moved.

"It doesn't look like anybody is there," Nikki offered.

Ludwig turned to face them all. "Now, listen. We need to go over there and try to find supplies out of those houses. We'll go in through the basement doors."

"What if the basement doors are locked?" Lise interrupted.

"Then we'll break a window," Kurt suggested.

Ludwig nodded at Kurt.

"We'll do whatever we have to do to get in. We need to find clothes. All of us must change."

Ludwig captured their attention. "Now, listen. Here is the plan. First Kurt and I will go through the house to make sure it's safe. Then, Kurt and I will keep a lookout while the rest of you go through the house and find what we need. You'll need to be extra careful as you walk inside because the houses have been damaged. You need to get clothes for us since we won't be able to search for ourselves."

They nodded their heads.

"Okay, you need to find food, matches and knives."

"And cooking and eating utensils," Kurt added.

"Yes, that's good," Ludwig commented. "Anything else?"

"Blankets and extra clothing and...," Kurt thought for a moment, "and backpacks to carry our things."

"Hats and scarves to cover our heads," Nikki added.

"Good, now can everyone remember those things?" Ludwig asked.

They responded positively and Ludwig smiled. "Remember, grab anything that might be useful to us."

"I'm scared; I don't want to go in," said Lise.

"We're all scared, but we'll watch out for each other," Ludwig persuaded her, and they began walking the dirt road to the houses.

In front of them was a group of ten houses situated next to the road. Bricks, glass and rubble lay scattered around. Some houses were missing part of their roofs and walls, exposing their interiors. As they neared the buildings, they stopped behind a tree. Ludwig turned to them. "Kurt and I are going to try to get in. Stay here and don't come until we call you."

They agreed.

Kurt and Ludwig ran to the cellar doors of the first home. They pulled at the slanted metal doors; luckily they opened. They looked around, quietly laid the doors to each side of the stairs, and went inside. Within a few minutes, Kurt popped his head up from the stairwell and waved for the others to come. Petr and the three girls ran, jumping over piles of debris. They skipped quickly down the concrete steps, stopping at the bottom. There was a thick cloud of dust darkening the cellar, and Kurt and Ludwig were coughing. The thick dust penetrated their nostrils and mouths. Petr and the girls started coughing. They could just barely see Ludwig bidding them to come over to him.

"The house is empty," he said as they neared. "Go up and find as much as you can. Kurt and I will let you know if someone is coming." Ludwig coughed again.

"Are you okay, Luddie?" Ursula asked.

"Yes," he coughed, "just hurry, and be careful." He pointed to the steps leading upstairs.

They heeded his request and bolted up the stairs. Once at the top, they found themselves in the kitchen. They inhaled deeply and looked at their surroundings.

"I'm so hungry," Petr said.

"No, to the bedrooms first," Nikki directed. "We must get a change of clothes."

They followed her through the kitchen and up the stairs to the bedrooms. Nikki and Petr went into a large bedroom to their left. To the right, Lise and Ursula saw a bedroom with painted yellow walls and floral curtains. They dodged inside, noticing two small beds.

Quickly Lise tore open the closet door while Ursula opened the dresser. "Look, I found underwear and socks," Ursula exclaimed.

"There are dresses and shirts in here; I hope they fit us," Lise said, as she took them off the hangers and threw them onto a bed. Ursula scooped out some clothing from the drawers and threw them on the bed, too. The girls excitedly rummaged through the pile for something that might fit them or the others. As Ursula pulled a blue dress from the pile, she smiled. It was a light blue, knee-length dress with a white lace pinafore. The short, puffy crinoline sleeves reminded Ursula of her ballerina tutu. There was even a flower shaped pocket on the pinafore for the prism necklace. She retrieved the necklace from the pocket of her uniform and laid it on the nearby dresser. She then untied her coat, plate and cup and let them fall to the floor. While she undressed, and as she pulled the uniform up over her head, she heard Lise walking toward the dresser.

"What's that?" Lise asked.

Ursula grabbed the blue dress and hurriedly pulled it down over her head.

"That is mine," Ursula said as she snatched the necklace away from Lise's gaze. "It was my Mumma's." She slid it into the flower pocket and tied her coat around her waist.

"I just wanted to look at it," Lise said hurtfully. "I don't have anything of my Mum's."

Ursula turned to ignore her and they walked back to the bed. They searched again through the pile of clothing. Ursula set aside a dress for Nikki. Lise picked out one for herself and began undressing.

"That dress you picked is too fancy," Lise contended as she buttoned her dress.

"Well I'm not changing," huffed Ursula.

Then Nikki and Petr entered the room.

"We found clothes for Kurt and Ludwig," Nikki said.

Petr had already changed into new clothing that was obviously oversized for him. But Nikki had not changed. Ursula held up the dress she had found for her.

"Here, Nikki, do you like this?" Ursula asked.

Nikki set the boys' clothing down.

"This will do just fine," Nikki said as she undressed and put it on. Nikki picked up some of the clothes lying on the bed. "Okay, now let's go downstairs and get food."

Ursula and Lise bent down to pick up their plates and cups. "No," Nikki stopped them. "Leave the plates here. They have Belsen marked on the back of them. We must leave all evidence of the camp behind."

They nodded in agreement and tied just the cup around their waists. Then they went downstairs into the kitchen.

The glass from the busted kitchen window shimmered in the sink and along the counter; there were bullet holes in the walls. Nikki laid her armful of clothing on the kitchen table. She opened the refrigerator door and a noxious odor invaded her senses.

"Oh my!" she exclaimed. "We can't eat anything from there."

They opened drawers and looked through cupboards, searching for everything Kurt and Ludwig had requested. Lise knelt down and pulled out a large stockpot from a bottom cupboard.

"Here's a nice cooking pot," Lise said.

"Too big," replied Nikki. Nikki stooped down to help Lise. They looked again in the cupboard and pulled out a medium sized pot and some spoons.

"We'll need these," Petr said. He held up two long pieces of cutlery, one in each hand.

"Oh, yes, come put them in the pot," Nikki said.

Ursula went to the other side of the kitchen, hunting through the cupboards. She laid all of her findings on the kitchen table—a few onions and potatoes, a can of beans, a can of broth, some tea bags, a can of cocoa and a box of matchsticks.

"That's all the food I can find," Ursula announced.

Lise, Nikki and Petr stopped their searching. They turned and looked at the table, their eyes gleaming with satisfaction.

"I think that's about all we can carry," Nikki said. She thought of Kurt and Ludwig in the basement below. "Let's take all these things to Kurt and Ludwig."

They gathered all that they had found and walked with arms overflowing down the basement stairs.

Kurt and Ludwig were at separate ends of the basement. Ludwig was standing on the top rung of a ladder while Kurt stood on a chair. They kept watch at two small dirty windows. When they heard the others approaching they got down from their positions. The opened basement doors had allowed the dust to dissipate and the children were no longer coughing. Eagerly Kurt and Ludwig walked toward them.

"What did you find?" Kurt asked.

"Clothes for both of you," Nikki said, as she handed each of them a shirt and a pair of pants. Kurt and Ludwig disrobed and dressed. The clothes didn't fit them well, but they still smiled with gratitude.

"Feels good to get out of that Nazi uniform," Kurt sighed.

"I'll say," Ludwig agreed.

"Excellent job, troops," Kurt playfully saluted them.

"Kurt and I haven't seen any signs of people, so we think it's safe to go on to the next house," Ludwig explained.

They went to the basement stairs that led outside. "Wait," Ludwig stopped the others, "let Kurt and I look out first."

Kurt and Ludwig walked up the steps, peeking out cautiously. "It's clear," he waved to them, and they ran up the steps. Outside in the daylight, just a few feet from the door, they dumped their armloads and sorted through the items.

"This is good, but we need more," Kurt offered.

"We can't carry all this while retrieving more. Let's leave everything here in a pile," said Ludwig. Ursula untied the coat from around her waist.

"Maybe it will look less suspicious with a German coat laying over it," Ursula suggested.

"Good idea, Urshey, now on to the next house," Ludwig motioned to Kurt. "Wait here," he told the younger ones.

Kurt and Ludwig ran to the next house and pulled at the basement doors. They swung open, and the boys hurried inside. Minutes later Kurt motioned for the other children to join them. Excitedly they ran. This basement was different from the previous one in that there was no thick cloud of dust, and the basement seemed more brightly lit.

"Okay troops, now go up and get more supplies," Kurt pointed to the steps.

They gladly obeyed his command. Once up on the first level, Nikki took over.

"Upstairs first, and we'll work our way down," Nikki said.

"We already changed clothes, why can't we just get food?" Lise asked.

"We still need to get hats for Kurt and Ludwig, and blankets and shoes," Nikki explained. "And it would be nice to find something to carry our things in."

They acceded to her advice and ran upstairs. Nikki, Petr and Ursula went into different bedrooms. Lise entered the bathroom, not really sure what she was looking for, but maybe something would catch her attention. *Aha!*

"Nikki, could we use this soap and towels?" Lise questioned.

Surprised, Nikki answered, "By all means, bring it along."

In the bedroom Ursula found a few hats, a backpack and a pair of shoes that fit her. Nikki exited the bedroom carrying a blanket, two scarves and a backpack.

"I found a backpack, too," Ursula held it up.

"Wonderful. Petr, what did you find?" Nikki called.

"Shoes and a hat." He came out with the hat on his head, wearing new shoes and carrying two other pairs.

"Good. Now let's go downstairs," Nikki exclaimed.

Lise, Petr and Ursula followed her down to the kitchen. "You two go into the front room and find the coat closet," Nikki said to the girls. "Look for shoes and backpacks."

They nodded and ran together into the living room. They threw open the closet door. Ursula grabbed shoes for Luddie and a backpack, while Lise grabbed another backpack. Then they ran back to the kitchen. Nikki and Petr looked in their direction as they entered the room. A few boxes and cans of food were strewn on the table, along with a can opener.

"Well that's all the food in the cupboard," Nikki announced.

"Look," Petr went to the table and picked up the can opener, "I found this."

"We certainly need that," Ursula grinned at Petr.

"Good, you found more backpacks. Let's fill them with these things," Nikki said.

They stuffed the backpacks with all that they had found and then went down into the cellar. Ludwig was perched upon an old chair and Kurt was atop a stepladder.

"Did you clean them out?" Kurt asked jokingly while climbing down.

"We took every bit of food out of the kitchen," Nikki declared.

"Our troops are doing well, Luddie," Kurt commented.

Ludwig came over to join them.

"Okay, let's put these things in the pile with the other stuff," Ludwig said.

They cautiously left the house's cellar with Kurt and Ludwig peeking out first before they all exited. When they reached their previous horde, they dumped the backpacks, gathering all the things into one pile. Petr looked longingly at the food.

"Can we eat now?" Petr asked.

"Just one more house," Ludwig said.

They covered everything with the German coat and walked to the next house. Once again, Kurt and Ludwig entered first, and when it was deemed safe, the other children were let in. They scurried through the home, finding another backpack, more pairs of shoes, blankets and more food, a large box of matchsticks and eating utensils. They even found more hats. With arms full, they trotted down to the basement to show Kurt and Ludwig. As they were looking over their new found possessions, they heard a noise outside.

"Shh, what was that?" asked Ludwig.

Kurt ran to the windows at the front end of the house and looked out. A military truck was coming down the road.

"Germans! Hide!" Kurt retorted.

Immediately the children dropped the items in their arms and scattered, finding cover where they could. Kurt stayed at the window, ducking out of sight as the truck puttered by. Cautiously, he spied out the window and watched them leave. When all was quiet, he spoke. "We need to get out of here, now!"

Without hesitation, they all sprang forth from their hiding places, gathering the things they had found. Kurt and Ludwig ran to the steps. They hushed the others as they warily climbed the stairs and peered out. Soon they signaled for the others to follow. All ran to their pile of stolen possessions.

"Our things are still here," Kurt remarked, as they gathered the spoils in their arms.

"Because the coat covered them," Ursula conjectured.

"Maybe so, Urshey, let's hurry," Ludwig replied. "Load the backpacks, quickly."

"Where should we go?" Nikki asked, throwing her filled backpack over her shoulder.

"Back to the woods, to follow the stream," Ludwig ordered.

With their backpacks full, they ran toward the woods. Once there, they followed the stream for a while and when they were far away from the dirt road and were no longer afraid, Lise and Petr asked, "When can we eat?"

"I'm hungry, too," Ludwig said. "As soon as we come to a clearing, we'll sit down and eat."

They murmured about their grumbling stomachs, but kept walking. After a short while, they came to a clearing. "Let's settle here."

They took their backpacks off and sat down in a circle, setting their backpacks in front of them.

"Well, let's see what's for dinner," Kurt jested.

They unzipped their bags and pulled out the food.

"I think we need to start a fire," Kurt said as he gazed at the boxed and canned foods in front of them. "Gather rocks and twigs."

In a hungered frenzy, they dashed about picking up stones and twigs and bringing them back to the clearing. Kurt and Ludwig piled the stones into a large circle and then laid the twigs on top. Kurt started the fire with the matchsticks, while Ludwig opened a can of broth and a can of vegetables and poured them into the cooking pot. Everyone used their new-found eating utensils as they dined on vegetable soup.

As they were eating, Ursula spied something unusual on Kurt's arm.

"Kurt, what's that on your arm?" Ursula asked.

Kurt held up his arm. A series of black numbers were tattooed onto his forearm.

"The Nazis put this on me at the other camp," Kurt said, raising his arm. "Then a few weeks later they sent me off to Bergen-Belsen; made me leave my parents," he sulked. "Does anyone else have one?"

The others shook their heads. They were silent for a moment.

"Maybe they did it to all the men first," Ludwig thought aloud. "Maybe they were going to give us one the next day."

"Did Poppa have one?" Ursula asked Ludwig.

"No."

They ate in silence.

"They didn't give me one," Petr broke the silence.

"Maybe they don't give you one if they know they're going to kill you. They brought me and my parents in from another camp. They took us to Belsen to die. They shot both my mum and my pop."

His face saddened and he dropped his head down. Then his head popped up and excitedly he added, "They thought I was dead too, because I pretended and hid." Silence again.

"They killed my parents, too," Lise said listlessly. "They like to make you watch."

"Enough of this!," Nikki cried. "I want to get out of Germany!"

"Well, then, we need to start walking," Ludwig said emphatically. Ludwig stood and took the empty cooking pot over to the stream. He filled it with water and doused the fire. Everyone stood up and filled their backpacks. They began walking again, following the stream.

"Didn't you say we needed to go west to get out of Germany?" Nikki questioned Ludwig.

"We need to go south first," Ludwig answered.

"When will we turn west?" Nikki asked impatiently.

Ludwig became irritated. "I don't know!"

"We will turn west when it's safe," Kurt added, trying to calm the flaring tempers.

Ludwig shook his head and Nikki sighed.

"Are your parents alive, Nikki?" Kurt asked.

"I don't know."

They walked in silence. Nikki glanced over at Ursula. She smirked at how the black, dingy hat she wore loudly disagreed with her dress.

"Ursula, that dress is too fancy," Nikki said.

"Well, I'm not changing," Ursula protested.

Ludwig chuckled to himself.

They walked for hours, following the stream.

"Are your parents alive, Ludwig?" Kurt asked.

"Only our father remains," he answered. "And yours?"

"I'm not sure, but I will find them when this war is over," Kurt said, his bottom lip trembling.

The sunlight was beginning to fade when luckily the forest was thinning again and they saw another group of houses ahead of them. These houses also showed signs of a military invasion.

"It's getting late, and we're all tired, let's sleep in one of those homes tonight," Kurt suggested.

"If it's safe," Ludwig added.

"Of course."

They stepped out of the woods, got closer to the homes and stopped.

"Let's just watch for awhile," Ludwig said.

They stood in silence observing the houses. There was no movement, no sound.

"I think it's safe. Do you agree?" Ludwig asked Kurt.

"Agree. Let's move, troops," Kurt said.

They walked down to the houses being careful not to stumble over the rubble. They tried to open the cellar doors of the closest home. It was locked. They went to the next house and the basement doors opened.

"We're going in first, stay close, we'll call for you," Kurt told the others as Ludwig and he entered the basement.

They waited.

"Come in," he called to them.

They wearily trudged down the steps. There was very

little light, just a few subtle rays from the dwindling day-light sun.

"I know it's hard to see," Ludwig began, "but try to find a place to bed down."

"I bet there are beds upstairs. Why can't we sleep in a bed upstairs?" Lise complained.

"It's safer down here," Kurt explained.

The children groped in the half darkness, pushing things out of their way, just enough to lay their bodies down. Spread on the floor as comfortably as possible, they wished each other goodnight.

As Ursula laid her head on her German coat pillow, a vision of Mumma flashed in her mind. Then she remembered.

"Luddie," Ursula prompted.

"Yes, Urshey."

"I didn't know Mumma was crippled."

Ludwig looked at Ursula in surprise.

"I thought you knew," he said to her.

"No," she replied, "Was she born that way?"

"No, she wasn't," Ludwig started. "When Mumma was a teenager she had a very bad horseback riding accident. The horse was frightened and bucked. She fell off, but her left foot was caught in the stirrup. The horse dragged her for quite a while until the leather strap broke."

"Wow, I never knew that," Ursula stared. "And I didn't know Mumma rode horses."

"Yes, she did," Ludwig said. "Poppa said she was very good with horses, until the accident."

Kurt was becoming too drowsy to keep his eyes open.

"Who wants first watch?" Kurt asked Ludwig.

"You sleep, I'll wake you when I'm tired," Ludwig assured him.

Kurt patted his shoulder and then settled down for a night's sleep.

Ludwig didn't mind taking first watch. He was wide awake, and couldn't figure out why. *I should be dead tired,* he thought. Maybe it was the excitement of freedom that kept him awake. Or maybe it was the weight of the responsibility of keeping himself and all the others alive. Or maybe it was Ursula's mentioning of Mumma. Whatever it was, he perched himself on the top of a ladder and watched fervently through the small basement window. *Very soon, the moon will be the only light.* He thought of the flashlight the kind mechanic had given him, but he didn't dare use it. Its' beam would surely give away their hiding place. He watched the sun sinking in the west and he thought, *Gee, even the sun wants to get out of Germany.*

Chapter Nine

The heat from the morning sun floated over Ludwig's cheek and whispered in his ear. He opened his eyes. He was lying on the floor a few feet away from the ladder, and Kurt was sitting on the top rung, looking out the small window. Ludwig shifted his gaze and watched a spider crawling on the floor in front of him. *I don't remember coming down from the ladder,* he thought. He turned his attention back to Kurt, who was smiling at him.

"Are you awake, now?" Kurt jested.

"How did I get on the floor? Did I fall asleep on the ladder?" Ludwig asked, pushing himself up.

"I'm not sure," Kurt began. "I woke in the middle of the night and came over to see if you were ready to be relieved. Your eyes were wide open, looking out the window, but when I talked to you, you wouldn't say a word. Just kept looking out the window. Never saw anything like it. I just pulled you down and set you on the floor. You fell asleep right away."

"Huh," Ludwig shrugged; he remembered none of it. He yawned and rubbed his eyes.

"Luddie," Kurt spoke apprehensively, "when this war is over, we will find our families and go back to our homes, right?"

Ludwig was quiet. *Will our homes be there?* He questioned himself. *What about Poppa and Sophus?*

"Yes, we will find them," he answered.

The other children were beginning to wake. Ludwig glanced at Ursula, who was stretching. She had slept curled up next to a tall cedar wardrobe, using the German coat as a pillow. The two other girls were close by her, stretching and yawning. Petr, just a few feet away, sat up and rubbed his eyes. Ludwig studied this newly formed group.

A band of six children randomly thrown together due to the most horrifying of conditions, he wondered if they all would make it out of Germany. Kurt seemed to have the survival skills needed, and he maintained a pleasant attitude which could help motivate and inspire the others. But Ludwig watched him move hastily, unthinkingly. *He means well,* Ludwig thought, *but he could unknowingly get us into trouble.* He thought of the other boy, Petr. He was visibly weakened by both concentration camps, yet life tenaciously clung to him. His spirit was stronger than what his emaciated form suggested. Was he spurred on by hatred, anger or fear? Ludwig wasn't sure. *He will do whatever he needs to do to survive.* Then he looked at the girls.

Ludwig didn't know how to respond to Nikki. She seemed to be helpful, but could quickly display a nasty temperament. Lise was intellectually bright but emotionally frail. *They will need to be watched with a keen eye, but I won't have to worry about Ursula.* He looked at Ursula and smiled. Ursula was tiny in stature, but she was tough and a fighter. *She will make it. She is quick-witted and stubborn, just like Mumma...was.* His throat tightened as his face heated. *Stop it,* he thought to himself, *I can't cry. I have to be strong for the others.*

"So, where do we go now, Luddie?" Kurt interrupted his thoughts.

"I say we ransack this house and a few more if we can get in. Then back to the forest to cook breakfast," Ludwig answered.

"Uh," moaned Nikki, "why can't we cook here in the kitchen?"

"Do you actually think there's petrol for the stove? And besides, the Germans believe these houses to be empty. You better believe they'll be coming back to make sure of it. We need to get in, get supplies and get out." Ludwig said. "We will eat in the woods where it's safer."

"Listen to Luddie, he's right," Kurt said, as he retreated down the ladder. "So come on, troops, go upstairs and see what you can find."

Petr and Ursula were the first to their feet, and they scurried to the stairs. Nikki and Lise begrudgingly shuffled their way upstairs. Once they were all upstairs, Kurt and Ludwig resumed lookout positions at the front and back of the house. Within half an hour the children ran back down into the cellar with their arms loaded. They divided the goods into the backpacks, gathered their things and went on to the next house. They ransacked through two more houses in the same manner. They were delighted with their finds, as they sat down in the basement of the third house to pack the stolen articles away.

Ursula counted the backpacks. "We only have five backpacks," she said, "One of us will have to go without." Their eyes shifted from the backpacks to each other.

"Ah, don't worry about me," Kurt obliged. "I can go without one. And besides, we'll probably find one for me later."

Kurt's nature was seemingly altruistic. People couldn't help but befriend him.

The children smiled at Kurt, and they continued filling the bags. They had obtained an abundance of provisions and soon realized that they couldn't zip the backpacks shut.

"Well, Luddie," Kurt said, looking at the half-zipped backpacks. "I think it's breakfast time."

Ludwig nodded in acknowledgment, as the group of children left the small parcel of bombed homes for the forest.

They found a safe place in the forest to settle down for a meal. While the girls gathered rocks and twigs, the boys took the extra twine that Kurt had brought from the camp and made a small trap. Kurt wrapped the twine into a circle with a slip knot. The boys laid it on the ground and hid behind some bushes, waiting for a rabbit to accidentally hop into the trap.

It was a sloppy operation. Kurt breathed nervously and Petr wiggled impatiently. Ludwig watched them both, chuckling to himself. Suddenly, Ludwig felt lightheaded. He sat back on his haunches. He was sitting with Kurt and Petr, but he felt like he was watching them from afar, as though they were actors in the theater and he was their audience. He watched the show.

The unsuspecting bunny hopped into the circle. Kurt pulled on the string just a little too late and caught the bunny by its tail. The bunny hopped about, trying to rid itself of the annoyance. Petr sprang up and jumped on top of the rabbit, clutched it to his chest and rolled on the ground. When he stopped rolling, he rose to his knees and held the bunny up by its throat in victory.

Ludwig's lightheaded feeling dispersed and Kurt and Ludwig jumped up and cheered. That day Kurt and Ludwig showed Petr how to gut and skin an animal.

"Does this mean I get to carry a knife?" Petr asked.

Kurt and Ludwig looked at each other.

"How old are you?" Kurt asked.

"Seven," he answered.

"Sorry, Petr," Ludwig said, "you're too young."

They put the cut up pieces of rabbit on long sticks and roasted them over the fire that they made. Lise complained, "How can you eat a little bunny rabbit?"

"Don't then, more for me," Ursula said, with gratifying moans at every bite. Lise grumbled, but as she watched the others eat the rabbit voraciously, she became curious. Her stomach rumbled.

"All right, I'll try a piece," Lise announced, as if her decision would please them. She grabbed a piece and ate it. When they were finished eating, Ludwig cleared his throat.

"We'll continue going south for a little while longer, then we'll turn west. It's safer to stay in the forest, but if we happen to come upon some more empty houses, we'll see what we can find."

"I agree with Luddie," Kurt said. "Let's clean up and get going. I still have the jug that the old man gave us. I'll go fill it at the stream."

"Be sure to get the water...," Ludwig started.

"Where it flows roughly over the rocks. Yes, I know," Kurt nodded to Ludwig.

Ludwig smiled.

Kurt walked over to the stream with the empty jug.

"Why does he need to get the water there, Luddie?" Ursula asked.

"Because that is where the water is the cleanest."

Ludwig flung the backpack over his shoulders. Having used some of their backpacks' contents, they had been able to rearrange things so that now the bags were able to be zipped closed.

Nikki eyed Petr as she zipped her backpack.

"Petr," Nikki approached him, "your accent sounds familiar. Are you from Poland?"

"Why, yes!" said Petr, smiling.

Gleeful recognition of shared citizenry broadened across their faces, and they held each other's hand as if touching a piece of home. They joined the others, walking hand in hand.

The children once again began their walk through the forest, following the stream. It was a hot and humid day. They were afforded some comfort by the hats and scarves that they wore to cover their baldness and by staying under the protective cover of the trees. After a few hours of walking, they saw another dirt road.

"Shall we follow the road, Luddie?" Kurt asked, gesturing toward the road.

"Yes," he replied.

As they stepped out of the forest, the midday sun blasted their faces.

"It's so hot," Lise complained.

"We knew that without you telling us," quipped Ursula.

Soon they came upon houses to the right of the road that looked untouched by the war.

"I wish we knew where we were," Ludwig wondered aloud.

Kurt nodded in agreement.

They kept walking. Soon the road sloped upward and turned left. Ahead they could see a road sign.

"Look," Kurt pointed, "we'll know where we are soon."

A white arrow was pointing to the left under a word, but the sign was too far away for them to read. As they eagerly quickened their pace, the letters became more legible. H...i...l...d...e....

Suddenly,..."Halt!" yelled a man's voice from a distance. The children turned their heads. A German soldier was walking toward them from the houses. In desperation, they knew they couldn't slacken their pace. They were getting closer to the sign and they just had to see the whole word - s...h...e...i....

"Who are you? Where are you from?" the soldier yelled as he walked up the hill on their right. He was about thirty yards away from them when Ludwig noticed that he was overweight. *He's far enough away, we may be able to outrun him,* Ludwig thought.

"Halt! Where are you going?"

Ludwig looked at the others.

"Go! Run into the woods," Ludwig charged them.

They turned and bolted into the forest. Petr was first to reenter the woods. Ludwig was amazed at his swiftness.

"Halt!" the soldier yelled repeatedly, as he climbed the hill and drew his gun from its holster.

The children ran as fast as they could, holding onto the straps as the backpacks flapped against their backs. The soldier was persistent. He was barely up the hill when he fired. Lise and Nikki screamed.

"Faster!" Ludwig yelled.

Ursula ran so fast that she couldn't see the ground. Her chest burned and she felt like she was in flight. In her peripheral vision she saw Lise and Nikki, their eyes bulging in fear. Ursula was scared, too, more frightened than she ever remembered. She imagined they were deer running from a hunter.

The soldier fired again and again as they ran deeper into the woods. The ground swelled upward, and after the children crested the embankment, Ludwig hoped they were now hidden from the soldier's view. They kept running. Eventually the gunfire relinquished as the soldier's shouts became fainter. They still ran for quite a distance before slowing their pace enough to talk.

"That...was...close!" Kurt yelled to Ludwig.

"Yes," Ludwig replied.

They stopped running. Petr and the girls stumbled to the ground. Kurt and Ludwig leaned against the trees, holding their stomachs. They tried to catch their breaths while Lise and Nikki sobbed.

"We...have...to...keep...walking," Ludwig panted.

Lise and Nikki cried louder.

"There...is...no...doubt," Ludwig swallowed, then continued, "he has told others about us. We must keep moving."

They struggled to their feet and continued on, breathing heavily. They walked wearily onward, still frightened by the event.

They walked quietly for about an hour.

"So, do we even know where we're going?" snapped Nikki, breaking the silence.

Ludwig gave her an irritated glare.

"For now, we are going straight. As the sun sets we will follow it." Ludwig said. "I wish we had been able to see the last letter of that sign."

"M," Petr said.

Everyone stopped. Ludwig looked at Petr in surprise. "Thank you, Petr!"

Petr nodded his head and Nikki hugged him. They repeated the letters, everyone speaking at once.

"H...i...l...d...e...s...h...e...i...m. Hildesheim!"

"Do you know how far Hildesheim is from Belsen?" Kurt asked Ludwig.

Ludwig looked down, twisting his mouth. He tried to recall the position of Hildesheim in relation to Belsen from the maps he memorized. He glanced at the five faces in front of him, anxiously awaiting his guidance. They trusted him, just as the mechanic who had risked his life trusted him. They believed him to be the knowledgeable one.

They trust me, I can't let them down, he thought. He couldn't remember, but looking skyward, he announced with a facade of confidence, "It is okay to go west now."

Their tightened, worrisome faces relaxed into smiles. Following Ludwig, they trekked through the forest, day after day, holding each other's hands in pairs: Nikki and Petr, Ludwig and Ursula, then Kurt and Lise.

They walked with trepidation during the day, listening for sounds of oncoming soldiers or airplanes overhead. If they heard anything suspicious, all the children would climb up the trees, or hide behind a bush, whatever was in the closest proximity. At night they slept on the forest floor, with Kurt and Ludwig alternating watch.

And so they walked for days, consuming the food in their backpacks. When the provisions were depleted, they ate berries and leaves. Kurt and Ludwig knew which plants were edible and which were poisonous. Luckily, apple and pear trees also dotted the landscape, and they picked nettle and dandelion leaves and boiled them in water. Many streams flowed through the forest, providing them fresh water for drinking and for their cooking pot. There was also an abundance of rabbits. The boys became skilled at trapping and preparing the rabbits, and Lise ate rabbit meat without complaining.

Once, while Kurt and Ludwig were watching from high up in the trees, they saw a wild turkey. Simultaneously, they clambered down.

"Did you see that, Luddie?" the excitement jumping from Kurt's eyes.

"Yes, let's get it!"

Luddie picked up a large stone and motioned for Kurt to follow him. Kurt gathered a stone and strode by Ludwig's side. They crept upon the turkey quietly, and when they were close enough, Kurt stood up and flung the stone at the turkey's head. The stone made direct contact and the turkey fell over. Ludwig ran over and smashed his stone down onto the turkey's head. Blood gushed from the head wounds as the two boys admired their catch. They laughed and patted each other on the back, then they sat down next to the dead turkey and began plucking its feathers.

"Oh, look!" exclaimed Nikki as she and the other children gathered around Kurt and Ludwig. "What a fine meal we'll have!"

She sat next to the boys and helped to pull out the feathers.

"Oh, good, I won't have to eat rabbit today," Lise said, as she also sat down and began to help pluck the feathers. Petr and Ursula sat down to help as well, and soon the turkey was featherless. Kurt held it up proudly. They took the turkey over to the stream and cleaned it in the water. Then Kurt and Ludwig cut it up into small pieces and boiled the meat.

"This is so good!" Ursula squealed.

The others nodded their heads as they filled their stomachs. They sat around the cooking pot, all day and all night, until the turkey meat was gone. Then they all fell asleep with their bellies full and more satisfied than any one of them had felt for such a long time.

The next day as they were walking, Lise discovered something.

"What's that over there?" Lise asked.

She pointed to a large, brown, box-shaped object in the distance. They ran to it. The object was covered with twigs and leaves. The children feverishly picked the debris off and threw it to the side. To their surprise, they uncovered a wooden wheelbarrow, its wheels half entrenched in the earth.

"This must have been here for quite some time," Kurt remarked.

"Looks like we'll have to dig it out," Ludwig said, as he searched his backpack for the knives. He pulled them out and handed one to Kurt.

Kurt and Ludwig began digging at the front wheel. The other children moved to the rear of the wheelbarrow. They retrieved some of the bigger sticks that they had cast away and began digging at the back wheels. Petr rocked the wheelbarrow as they dug. Eventually, it moved. They tugged at the handles and pulled it free. Lise, Nikki and Ursula cheered and clapped. Dirt was packed inside.

"Let's take it over to the stream and wash it out," Kurt suggested.

They pushed it over to the stream, laid it down on its side and let the water run in. After they cleaned it as well as they could, they noticed that it was missing some of the boards on the bottom. Lise and Nikki looked dismayed.

"It's still useable," Ludwig said.

They smiled.

Only three of the five backpacks could fit into the wheelbarrow, so Ludwig and Nikki agreed to carry theirs. Kurt and Ludwig took turns pushing the wheelbarrow as they headed through the forest again.

And so they walked for two more days. Then the forest thinned out. Ahead of them they saw a few farmhouses with workers in the fields gathering crops.

"I have an idea," started Kurt, his eyes flashing with excitement. "We can go to one of those farms and ask if they need help. We'll work for food."

His zeal excited the children. Lise and Ursula hopped up and down.

"Yes, let's go," they said together.

"Yay. No more rabbit!" Lise exclaimed.

They started walking.

Suddenly, Ludwig held up his hand.

"Wait," Ludwig stopped them. "It's getting late," he pointed to the dropping sun. "We should sleep here overnight, where it's safe. Kurt and I will keep watch for signs of any military. We'll go to the farm tomorrow if it's safe."

The children sighed and lowered their heads; their heightened expectations now quenched. Still, they knew that Ludwig was right.

So, with the sun setting beyond them, they settled down under the safe canopy of the trees for the night. They used their backpacks as pillows.

Ursula used the coat as a pillow, and as she lay there she dipped her hand into her dress pocket to make sure the prism necklace was still there. She ran her fingers over the rough side, then the smooth side. *Maybe tomorrow will be our good day.* She smiled with anticipation as she drifted off to sleep.

Chapter Ten

Ursula was awakened by the chirping of birds. She heard Kurt and Ludwig talking. "You and I should go together," Ursula heard Kurt say.

"Okay, and everyone else will wait here," Ludwig replied.

"Yes, they should," Kurt agreed.

"Why, why do we need to wait here?" Ursula asked, sitting up.

The other children were waking. Ludwig walked over to Ursula and placed his hand on her shoulder.

"In case we don't come back," Ludwig answered.

Dread trickled down Ursula's spine.

"Don't go, Luddie," she clutched his arm.

"We should be alright," he said, while stroking her bare head. "Kurt and I have been watching, and we haven't seen any sign of German soldiers."

The others were sitting up and listening. Ludwig looked around and spoke to all of them.

"Kurt and I are going over to the farm to see if they will give us work. All of you are to stay hidden behind the trees until we come back." Ludwig stood up. "If we don't come back, keep going that way," he pointed.

"Why wouldn't you come back?" Lise asked in a worrisome tone.

"Don't worry," Nikki said as Petr clung to her, "they will come back."

The children scurried to hide behind the trees. They watched Kurt and Ludwig walk toward the farm. Ursula's knees trembled as she wrapped her arms around a young tree.

The farmland and the backs of the houses faced the woods. As Kurt and Ludwig neared the closest house, they turned the corner to go to the front and disappeared from the children's sight. Ursula drew a deep breath. *Please come back, Luddie.*

They waited almost a quarter of an hour and then saw Kurt and Ludwig walking back around the corner of the house.

"Whew!" Ursula exhaled loudly.

The boys ran to the woods with grinning faces.

"C'mon," Kurt and Ludwig summoned as they neared, "they have work for us!"

The children eagerly jumped out from behind the trees and joined Kurt and Ludwig. They walked excitedly. Nikki and Ursula pushed the wheelbarrow, while Petr and Lise skipped beside.

"No more dead bunnies!" Lise exclaimed.

"I thought you didn't mind eating rabbit now," Ursula contested.

"I was just pretending," Lise snubbed.

Ludwig almost laughed at their enthusiasm.

"Now, listen," Ludwig instructed as they walked. "Don't tell them that we're Jews, or that we've escaped from Belsen. In fact, try not to talk at all."

Ludwig glanced at them as they walked. They all wore either a hat or a scarf to cover their heads. *Six bald children traveling alone.* Ludwig sighed. He knew the farmers weren't stupid. *They will figure out who we are and where we are from,* Ludwig thought. *It's just a matter of time. I wonder how long they will let us live.*

The farmer and his wife stood outside on the back porch of the house, watching the approaching group. Their big, black dog barked, and the farmer held the leash as the dog jumped.

"Well, well," the woman said as she stepped down from the porch. "Isn't this an interesting little troupe?" The woman smiled as she looked over the children, but to Ursula it was a disquieting, eerie smile. "Look, Leonard, they have a little wheelbarrow."

"Yes, I see that, Mathilda," Leonard said, trying desperately to restrain the dog. The dog barked and jumped. "Calm down, Pepper!"

Leonard started down the stairs with Pepper. "He's just excited to have company." He bent down and freed the dog's collar from the leash. "Don't worry, he's friendly."

Pepper ran to the children and sniffed them up and down, one by one. His tail wagged so hard that it thumped audibly against the sides of his body. The dog was almost as big as Lise, and when Pepper bounced against her and sniffed and licked her face, she was a little overwhelmed. "Oh, it's okay, little one, he's just checkin' you over."

"Well, that wheelbarrow isn't big enough," Mathilda said, getting back to business. "Follow me, there's some in the barn for you to use."

They followed Leonard and Mathilda to the barn with Pepper bounding alongside. Every so often he would jump onto one of the children. Lise uttered a whimper of dissatisfaction when he bounced against her.

Ludwig believed Leonard and Mathilda to be in their fifties, due to their graying hair and the wrinkling of their skin. They were both slightly overweight, and Leonard's body swayed with each step.

Ursula surveyed the farm as they walked. Tall stalks of corn rose proudly in the heat next to row after row of green vegetation. The leaves seemed to be waving to her with the gentle breeze.

It was a moderate sized white barn, and since the farm was just for produce and no livestock, the barn was filled with tractors and accompanying equipment.

"As you can see, we store the hay and straw in the loft and the other crops get stored here," Leonard said, pointing to the one side of the barn.

"Here are the wheelbarrows," Mathilda said, "We'll show you which crops to pick first."

Ursula and Nikki pushed their small wheelbarrow into a corner of the barn and set it down. Ludwig and Kurt picked one of the farmer's wheelbarrows from the barn, and all of the children followed Leonard, Mathilda and Pepper outside.

The farmers showed the children the vegetation that was ready to be harvested. The children worked all day digging up potatoes and carrots, and cutting cabbage. They'd throw the vegetables into the wheelbarrow, and at the end of the day, there was a large pile of produce in the barn that they had collected.

As the sun was setting, the exhausted children sat on the ground inside the barn, waiting for the farmers to come and see their work. Soon Leonard and Mathilda, with Pepper by their side, came into the barn.

"Well, Mathilda, look at all they did," he said, looking over the pile of food. She nodded in agreement.

"Good job," she said to the children. "Pick what you want to eat."

She saw Lise and Petr lying on the ground. "Don't sleep there, go up in the loft and sleep on the straw."

"You mean we can stay here?" Ludwig asked in surprise.

"Sure, why not? You got somewhere else to go?"

She glared at the children, taunting them for an answer. "Didn't think so. C'mon, Leonard."

She turned toward the door. "We'll be back with some blankets."

The children ran to the pile of vegetables and excitedly picked what they wanted to eat. They took the food to the water pump just outside the barn door and washed the vegetables. They said grace, ate and marveled at how wonderful it tasted.

The farmers came back carrying a blanket for each child. They each took a blanket and climbed the ladder to the loft where they put their blankets down over the straw. They then lay on the blankets.

Ludwig stood and stretched.

"Luddie, do you think we need to stay awake and keep watch?" Kurt asked.

"No, Kurt, I don't think that will be necessary," Ludwig replied, as Kurt lay down.

Moonlight streamed through the open window. Ludwig inspected the area, making sure everyone was safe and comfortable.

"Luddie," Ursula gestured for him to come near. He stooped down.

"Yes, Urshey," he replied, "is something wrong?"

"I want to show you something," she said as she reached into her pocket and pulled out the prism necklace. It sparkled in the moonlight. Ludwig gasped with surprise. Yes, he remembered Mumma wearing the crystal prism necklace. Yes, he remembered as a small boy sitting on Mumma's lap and learning the prism principles. He touched the necklace as if through it he could touch Mumma. He blinked back the tears that were welling in his eyes.

"Don't ever lose it, Urshey," Ludwig said. He closed her hand over the necklace.

"I won't," she promised.

He hugged her. Ursula put the necklace back safely into her pocket and lay down for the night. Ludwig walked over to his blanket. As he lay there, he couldn't stop thinking about Mumma, Poppa, Hanrie and Sophus. He cried silently in the night, tears rolling down his face onto the blanket, saturating it.

Morning came, and the creaking of the barn door awakened the children.

"Good morning," Leonard called.

Pepper barked.

The aroma of fried eggs seduced their nostrils. They sat up with beaming faces. Putting on their hats and readjusting their scarves, they scrambled to the ladder.

Mathilda carried a large skillet and six forks. A small inner tube stood propped against a wall. She kicked it so it fell flat on the ground, and then she laid the skillet on top of it.

"Here's your breakfast," she said as she handed the forks to the children. "When you finish, put the skillet on the back porch."

"Pepper likes to lick it clean," Leonard announced.

Mathilda glowered at him.

"Then get to work. C'mon, Leonard," Mathilda commanded.

They turned and went back to the house. The children sat around the inner tube, feverishly consuming the eggs. When they were finished, Ludwig gathered the forks.

"Okay, everyone, now get the wheelbarrow and go out and start," Ludwig picked up the empty skillet. "I'll take this to the house, then meet you out in the field." The children bustled with activity, while Ludwig carried the skillet and forks to the house.

Pepper stood on the porch, watching Ludwig, waiting for the skillet's arrival. His tail was motionless, but his head moved inquisitively. Ludwig felt uneasy as he approached the porch and set the skillet down. Pepper's muzzle immediately scoured the pan, with his long tongue furiously knocking the forks out. They toppled down the steps. Ludwig gathered them up, and as he leaned forward to put the forks on the porch, Pepper stopped. With his muzzle still in the pan, his eyes became fixed on Ludwig. He growled and bared his teeth, his growling becoming louder and more ferocious with each second that Ludwig stood there.

Slowly, Ludwig backed away. Pepper calmed and continued with his feast.

Whew! Ludwig felt uncomfortable, like someone was watching him. But as he looked around, he saw no one. Pepper was engrossed with the skillet, so Ludwig turned and walked through the barn to the field.

The children worked all day and into the evening gathering the crops. Afterwards, they sat exhausted inside the barn. Leonard, Mathilda and Pepper came into the barn. Leonard was carrying a brown paper bag.

"Well, we can see that you are a mighty fine group of workers," Leonard said. Leonard walked toward Kurt. "Boy, I see that you don't have one of these."

Leonard pulled a backpack out of the bag and held it up toward Kurt. "You can have this one if you want, I don't need it anymore."

"Really?" Kurt's heart flushed with gratitude. He took the backpack. "It's wonderful. Thank you, thank you very much, thank you."

"Ah, it's nothing, boy, you just use it and enjoy it." Leonard patted Kurt on the back.

"Well, it's evening," Mathilda interrupted, seemingly upset, "you'd better eat and get straight to bed." She pointed to the pile of vegetables, and then the loft. "Morning comes real soon. C'mon, Leonard."

They left the barn with Pepper by their side. Ludwig was puzzled by Mathilda's demeanor. *Poppa said there are a lot of unhappy people in the world,* he thought, *but I wonder if there is more to it than that.* He shrugged, then sat with the rest of the children as they ate their dinner of fresh vegetables. His belly full, he climbed to the loft for bed. He watched Kurt's blissful face as he slept curled up with the backpack.

The children stayed at the farm for the rest of harvest time. They were greeted by Leonard, Mathilda and Pepper every morning with a hot breakfast. During the day, they worked long, hard hours in appreciation for the food and a safe place to sleep. But the harvesting time was coming to an end, and one day, in the early evening, out in the field, Ludwig and Ursula were alone at the end of a row of vegetation.

"Luddie," Ursula began.

"Yes, Urshey."

"I think Mathilda hates us."

"Oh, Urshey, some people are just not happy people," Ludwig said, remembering Poppa's words.

"No, Luddie, this is different. She looks at us with hatred in her eyes. I see it; I can feel it. She scares me."

Ludwig was silent. He held the same apprehension.

"Luddie," she stared directly into his eyes, "I don't think we're going to be alive much longer." Her conviction frightened him.

"Luddie, Urshey!" Kurt waved to them from across the field. "Let's stop for the day."

They waved in return.

"Let's go, Urshey, we'll make mention of this tonight," Ludwig promised.

After they had eaten their dinner of vegetables, Ludwig confided in the others. "Look, Urshey and I think there's something peculiar about Leonard and Mathilda."

Ursula sat by his side, nodding in agreement.

"What do you mean?" asked Kurt, obviously offended.

"We mean, we think something bad is going to happen to us," explained Ludwig.

"Like what? You're being ridiculous," inflected Kurt. "They have helped us. They've given us a place to stay and breakfast every morning. And they gave me a backpack."

"We're not being ridiculous," Ludwig entreated. "We don't trust them."

"Well, I think the both of you *are* being ridiculous, and I'll prove it. Tonight, when it gets darker, I'll go over to the house. I'll listen at the window and see if they're saying anything about us," Kurt defended.

Lise, Nikki and Petr looked at each other in confusion, not knowing who to believe.

"They don't mean to do us any harm. You'll see."

After it became darker, Kurt opened the barn door slowly so it wouldn't creak. He looked at the house. One room on the bottom floor was lit, and he could see shadows of Leonard and Mathilda. He stepped outside and tip-toed toward the house, grateful that it was a cloudy night. He advanced to the lit room and knelt down at the window. Their voices resonated from within.

"Well, I told you not to become attached to those children," Mathilda said.

"Can't we just tell them to leave?" asked Leonard.

"For the last time — no! We are calling the SS tomorrow. We have neighbors, and I know they've seen the children. If they call the SS before we do, they'll be burying our corpses, too. Do you understand me?"

"Yes, Mathilda."

"Let's go to bed. C'mon, Leonard."

Kurt sat for a moment, astonished. *Ludwig and Ursula were right.* His spirit was crushed. *I thought they liked us. I thought they liked me.*

He waited for the light to go out and to hear their fading footsteps. He then ran back to the barn.

"Quick, pack your things!" Kurt announced. The children jumped to their feet.

"Kurt, what did you hear?" Ludwig asked.

Kurt's gaze dulled.

"They're calling the SS tomorrow. They're coming to get us and take us away! I can't believe it. Why would they do that?" Kurt looked at the others, his eyes dazed. "They fed us every day and gave us a place to sleep. Why would they call the army on us now?"

"They don't have a use for us anymore. Harvest time is over."

Ludwig and the other children retrieved their backpacks, filling them with various things from the barn. Kurt watched them in dismay as they rushed about.

I don't believe it, Kurt thought. *Leonard won't let them hurt me.*

"I'm not going," Kurt responded. Ludwig was incredulous. The children stopped packing and gaped at Kurt.

"What!" Ludwig cried.

"I'm staying here," Kurt insisted. He thought of the hot breakfasts, the straw bed in the loft, and the backpack. "All of you can go, I'm staying here."

"And what will you do when the soldiers get here?" Ludwig asked.

"I'll tell them I'm German. I have blue eyes and blond hair," Kurt protested.

Ludwig marched up to Kurt and pulled the hat off his head. He put his hands on Kurt's shoulders and shook him. "You have no hair! Kurt, we have to leave! If you stay here, you are putting yourself and all of us in danger!"

Ludwig turned to pick up his backpack. Kurt stood silent, baffled by the events. The others continued packing.

"I thought they liked us," Kurt replied.

Ludwig noted his dejected expression.

"It's not him, it's her," Ludwig explained.

Leonard's and Mathilda's rejection and deceit hit Kurt like a punch to his abdomen. Kurt watched everyone filling their backpacks to leave. He felt his stomach contents churning.

Enraged, Kurt walked over to a wheelbarrow. "Well, if that's the way it has to be, we're taking this with us," he said as he pulled it away from the wall.

"Let's fill it with vegetables," suggested Nikki.

"Yeah!" the children agreed.

"And straw and blankets," said Ursula.

"Yeah!"

They climbed up to the loft and filled their arms with straw and the blankets. They put these in the wheelbarrow and then filled it the rest of the way with vegetables. They foraged through the barn and gathered things that they thought might be useful to them, stuffing their backpacks. Then they were finished.

"All right, let's go, and be very quiet," Ludwig directed.

They left the barn and went to the forest. After they had made it to the safety of the woods, Kurt turned to them all and spoke.

"Now, stay here," he rummaged through his backpack, pulling out a small box, "I'll be right back."

"Kurt, what are you doing?" Ludwig asked.

"You'll see," Kurt grinned. "Don't worry, I am coming back."

They watched Kurt run back to the barn. He went inside. Minutes later he left the barn and came running back to the others. "Ha, ha, ha, they'll know better than to mess with us," Kurt said as he held up and shook the box of matchsticks.

"Kurt, what did you do?" they all asked him.

He pointed to the barn. "Patience, now. Watch."

At first all they saw was a yellow-red spark here and there. Suddenly, flames erupted from the building and smoke billowed upwards. The children watched, smiling and laughing.

Chapter Eleven

In triumph, they watched the burning barn for a while. "They'll be looking for us," Ludwig warned.

Ludwig still carried the flashlight that the mechanic had given him. He pulled it out of his backpack. Luckily, he had found batteries in the barn, and he installed two new ones while throwing the old two to the ground. They huddled together while Kurt and Nikki pushed the wheelbarrow behind them.

They walked by the small circle of light emitted by the flashlight for about an hour, and then came to a clearing in the woods. Ludwig turned the flashlight off and they settled down for the night, with Kurt and Ludwig alternating watch.

The next morning they began walking in a westerly direction through the forest. Before the sun had reached its midday position, they saw a small structure in front of them.

"Luddie, what could that be?" questioned Ursula.

"It looks like a little house," Ludwig answered.

They gasped in amazement.

"I wonder if anyone lives there," Nikki said aloud.

"It looks abandoned," Kurt replied, the overgrown weeds surrounding the structure lending credence to his observation.

"Might be abandoned, might not be. Let's go see," Ludwig said.

As they approached, they saw that the front door was invitingly wide open. They eagerly entered.

It was a small, brick hut approximately twelve feet square. It had one wooden door with an interior latch, and one small window. There was a shelf on one of the walls, and two items sat on the shelf: a metal stein and a ball of twine. The floor was made of concrete, and in one corner of the hut there was a chimney stack. The chimney stack started halfway up the wall and projected out through the roof. Beneath the chimney stack were three metal grates, positioned parallel one to the other. Two edges of the grates were cemented into the wall to support them. Ursula imagined that they were used for cooking. Underneath the grates was a hole in the concrete floor. There was a small pile of wood next to the hole. A musty smell permeated the shack, and as Ludwig investigated the walls he noticed a small amount of moss growing between the bricks along the floor, indicating water leakage.

"Do you think someone still lives here?" Nikki asked.

"Even though it seems this hut is abandoned, we still need to survey the area to see if there are any signs of the SS around," Ludwig answered.

"Ludwig is right," Kurt came up behind him and patted him on the shoulder, "as always."

"So, let's investigate," Petr said impatiently.

"We will need a way to mark our path," Ludwig said. "I grabbed a pair of cutting shears from the barn. Give me something to cut up into small pieces, like a blanket or towel."

"I have a towel," Lise said. She rummaged through her backpack and found a towel. She handed it to Ludwig who then cut it up into many small strips.

"As we walk, we will tie these strips around tree branches to mark our way so we can come back to this hut," Ludwig explained.

Though the house looked abandoned, they took their wheelbarrow and their backpacks with them, just in case the hut's owner came back. Walking approximately fifty yards around the hut in different directions, they created a perimeter with the towel pieces. There were no signs of other people.

"It's getting late, Luddie. How about heading back to the hut?" Kurt suggested.

"Yes, I'm sure everyone is hungry," Ludwig stated.

"Yes!" they harmonized.

"Do you think it's safe to stay the night in the hut?" Kurt asked.

"So far, I'd say yes," Ludwig replied.

Lise and Nikki smiled at each other. They followed the towel strips back to the hut. A stream trickled its way close to the hut, so they washed their vegetables in the stream and filled their cooking pot with water. Inside the hut, Lise and Nikki divided the straw equally among them, piling straw on opposite sides of the hut.

"Boys sleep on this side, and girls sleep on this side," Nikki clarified.

"Do you think this is safe for cooking?" Kurt asked, pointing to the grates.

"Let's try it. Bring out your matchsticks," Ludwig answered. "Urshey, hand me your coat."

"Okay, but why?" she asked.

"The light of the fire may bring attention to us. I want to put your coat in the window to block the light."

Ludwig stuffed Ursula's coat into the frame of the small window. Then Kurt and Ludwig put a few pieces of straw into the hole in the floor to start a fire. As the kindling lit, they used the wood that was lying next to the hole to create a stronger fire. The grates seemed sturdy enough to bear weight, so they put their cooking pot filled with water and vegetables on the grate over the fire. Eagerly they watched the vegetables floating in the water, when suddenly they realized something was amiss. The aroma rose, filling their nostrils, but somehow the smoke that was also rising began filling the shack. The smoke rolled up the chimney but billowed angrily downward, refusing to empty itself out the smokestack. Suddenly the children found themselves smothered in a grey cloud. Heaving and coughing, they stumbled outside, leaving the door open as the smoke freed itself.

"Luddie, what happened?" Kurt asked.

"My guess is something is clogging the smokestack. We won't be able to cook inside anymore. As soon as the smoke clears we will douse the fire."

"I hope this smoke doesn't bring attention to us," commented Nikki with Petr clutching her side.

How true, Luddie thought.

"C'mon everyone, to the stream for water," Ludwig said. They fetched their cups and the gallon jug and walked over to the stream. After filling them, they came back to the hut and, holding their noses, went inside to pour the water on the fire. More smoke billowed upward, forcing the children to run outside. Kurt carried the pot of vegetables.

"We'll have to finish cooking this outside," Kurt said. So they finished cooking the meal outside, and when they had ladled portions for themselves into their cups, they looked longingly at the shack.

"Can we sleep inside the hut?" Lise asked.

They gazed at each other. Somehow, Lise had spoken their silent desire.

"Positively," answered Ludwig.

Happily, they all headed indoors.

The cooked meal, the roof over their heads, and the ability to lock the door gave the children security. It almost seemed like a real home.

But the people left, thought Ludwig, and suddenly the scenes from Glashütte, his hometown, flashed into his mind. The horrible memories of people crying as they were being pulled out of their homes by the Nazis and pushed into military trucks haunted him. People were taken away and never seen again. As he watched from the safety of his living room window, speculating about where they were taken, Ludwig had then hoped it would never happen to him and his family. He shook his head.

When they finished eating, Nikki said, "Winter is coming."

Ludwig stared at her, wondering why she mentioned that.

"Why don't we just stay here for the winter?" Nikki continued.

Lise, Petr and Ursula nodded their heads. Ludwig was aghast.

"We need to get out of Germany as soon as possible!" Kurt agreed with Ludwig.

"But with the cold and the wind and the rain and the snow, we could die on the way!" Nikki pleaded.

The boys were silent. Ludwig thought, *She is right. It must be November by now and the elements could be harsh. How much more can they take?*

Ludwig glanced at Kurt who shrugged his shoulders.

"She has a point, Luddie," Kurt said. The children looked at each other excitedly.

"I guess we can stay here for the winter, as long as the SS doesn't come near," Ludwig decided.

Lise and Nikki clapped.

"Maybe we can try making just a small fire," he continued, "you know, for heat, since we are staying here for the winter."

With just a few pieces of straw and twigs, they started a fire in the hole. They waited to see if the smoke would rise into a billowing cloud again, but it didn't. A few small flames playfully flickered over the twigs, their light dancing on the children's faces. Kurt and Ludwig looked at each other, nodding in satisfaction.

"Looks like if we keep the fire small we won't get smoked out," Kurt suggested.

"It appears so," agreed Ludwig.

Then they bedded down for the night, girls on one side, boys on the other, while Nikki serenaded them with stories of Poland, her homeland.

Days passed and they ran out of provisions.

"We must go out and see if there are houses or farms close to us," Ludwig began. "We need to find food and straw. We'll start early in the morning and come back here at night."

So, in the chill of the winter months, they headed out each day in exploration. Ludwig and Kurt had agreed that they would only walk until the late afternoon, and then head back to the hut, regardless if they had found anything or not. Fortunately, they did find provisions. They found that if they headed in a southern direction, there was farmland. If they headed north or west, there were more bombed houses. In this manner, they were able to furnish themselves with the supplies they needed. Some days they would walk to a farm where they would steal vegetables and straw for their bedding and fire. Other days they would scour the bombed houses, searching for food and clothing. They walked silently and watched carefully, keeping alert and scrambling to hide if any German soldiers neared.

One day, as they were leaving the houses, they walked by a huge ditch with a large pile of turned up soil next to it. It looked like freshly dug excavation.

"Luddie, what could that be?" Ursula asked.

"I don't know," he replied. "Let's look."

They walked over. As they got closer their nostrils were stung by a horrific odor, and they heard a low, buzzing sound.

"Ew, what is that smell?" Lise asked.

"I've smelled that before," Nikki acknowledged.

They walked closer and looked down into the hole. Lise and Ursula yelped. Dozens of decomposing bodies lay strewn in the bottom, some clothed, some not. Flies and maggots dotted the bodies, while rats scampered across. It was a mass grave.

Ludwig and Kurt looked around, alarmed.

"Quick, let's get out of here," Kurt said. They turned quickly.

"We won't come this way again," Ludwig stated.

Lise and Ursula cried as they walked away. The image of Little Hanrie's lifeless body flashed into Ursula's mind. She cried louder.

"Shh, girls, I know this is horrible, but we must be quiet. The SS may still be around." Ludwig and Kurt held their fingers up to their pursed lips.

How, Luddie, Ursula screamed silently, *how can I get Hanrie out of my head? And Mumma...MUMMA!* Ursula closed her eyes. She bowed her head and shook it. *Maybe I can shake them out!* Ursula clamped her hand over her mouth to muffle her cries as they hurried back to the hut.

When they arrived back at the hut, Lise and Ursula exhaustedly slumped to the ground.

"I will never forget that," Lise said between breaths.

Kurt looked up into the sky.

"Those clouds look like snow clouds," Kurt announced. "Gather as many sticks as you can," he charged everyone.

He picked up a stick about one inch in diameter. "About this size. As many as you can find."

"Why?" asked Ludwig.

"You'll see," Kurt smiled.

Curious, they complied with Kurt's request and gathered armloads of sticks. They took them into the hut and laid them down in a pile under the window.

"That's a big pile of sticks, Kurt. Why do you want them?" Ludwig asked again.

"Nothing right now, let them sit there. I'm too hungry to work with them, but tomorrow, you'll see."

They stuffed Ursula's coat in the window and ate their meal. Then they lay down on their straw beds. When they awoke the next day, they opened the door, revealing that an inch of snow had covered the ground overnight.

"Wow!" Lise and Ursula chanted.

"Aha, I knew it," Kurt exclaimed with glee.

He grabbed the twine from the shelf.

"I know I have more string in here," Kurt said, as he searched through his backpack. "Yes." He pulled the ball of string out then sat down next to the pile of sticks with the two balls of string. "We need to go outside, right?" he asked Ludwig, as he began to lay the sticks in a flattened row.

Ludwig nodded.

"We'll need snowshoes."

They gathered around Kurt and watched as he lay the sticks in parallel groupings and tied them together. When he was finished, he had created twelve miniature rafts. "All we need to do is tie one to the bottom of each foot," he demonstrated.

"That's wonderful, Kurt," Ludwig said, patting his back. "Thank you."

"Yes, thank you," the others replied, as they tried on the snowshoes.

So now they were able to venture out each day, whatever the weather, wearing the snowshoes Kurt had made. And during the long winter nights, they stayed in the hut huddled together in their blankets around the small flame.

Winter had come quickly, but gently, with only one snowfall that persisted for a week. But even with the mild winter, food was scarce. The snow melted away, but the edible plants were dormant, and notably less rabbits hopped about. If the children caught one rabbit, they considered it a feast. They battled continuous hunger pangs and, some days, had nothing to eat at all. Their energy dwindled. Still, Ludwig insisted they go out each day in search of provisions.

"I don't want to go," Lise moaned. She sat against the hut's wall, clutching her stomach. "I'm too tired, and I hurt. We won't find anything and the farmers will chase us off."

Ludwig turned away from her.

She was right. They had despoiled the outlying bombed homes, and they were now as empty as their stomachs. Last time they went to a farm, the farmers ran them off, cursing and threatening them.

Ludwig was tired, too. He didn't want to go outside of the hut either.

I know there's nothing outside to eat, but we have to look, we have to try. We have to do something besides just sit here, thought Ludwig.

They were running low on matchsticks, so they tried to keep a constant but low fire burning. "We have to get more straw for the fire," he told Lise.

"Oh," Lise groaned, "why can't I just stay here?"

"We have to stay together," Ludwig explained.

"Come on, Lise," Nikki offered Lise her hand. "I'll help you."

Luckily for the children, spring was impatient. Sadly, it rained almost every day. Ludwig was amazed at how sturdy the hut was as the rain pummeled against it. Ursula's coat in the window retained some condensation, and just a tiny amount of water leaked inside on the floor where the moss grew.

"Now that winter is over, we can concentrate on getting out of Germany," Kurt said.

"Yes, we need to leave soon," Ludwig agreed, "just as soon as the rainy weather stops."

One day, as they sat in the hut, Ursula waited quietly for the rain to stop. Then she approached her brother.

"Luddie, I need to go to the bathroom," she told him.

Ludwig reached into his backpack and pulled out one of the knives.

"Okay, let's go," he said as they walked outside of the hut together. They had made rules—no one was to be alone at any time, any place, no matter what. When someone had to relieve themselves, either Kurt or Ludwig was to go with them. When one of them wanted to wash themselves, they would use the tiny bits of soap that Lise had found and bathe in the cold stream water with Kurt or Ludwig standing by.

They had specific areas they deemed safe for bathroom use. Ludwig and Ursula walked to one of them now. It was a large bush just over an embankment, a short distance from the hut. Everyone knew the procedure. Kurt or Ludwig would climb up the tree next to the bush. After they got to the top and scanned the territory, Kurt or Ludwig would whistle if it was safe.

Ursula stood at the bush quietly waiting for Ludwig's whistle. Finally he whistled and Ursula commenced to relieve herself. Just as she finished, she heard a twig snap. Ursula jumped in fright.

"No, no, don't be afraid little girl," a voice sounded. It was a German soldier. He was smiling at her, but his eyes, protuberant and maniacal, scared her. Ursula was so frightened that she couldn't move. She tried to scream, but her throat tightened as she gasped for air.

He came closer while his hand unbuckled his belt. "That's right, don't move." He reached for her arm and grabbed it.

Then, suddenly,…

"No!" Ludwig yelled as he jumped from the tree. The German soldier looked up and saw Ludwig with the knife in his hand about to fall on him. The soldier quickly reached for his own knife and scratched it across Ursula's forearm. She cried out.

Ludwig fell on top of the soldier, knocking him to the ground. He sat on top of the fallen soldier and plunged the knife into his chest. Kurt exploded out from behind Ursula. He joined Ludwig on top of the soldier and pushing the soldier's head to one side, he stabbed him in his neck. The other children ran over. They picked up stones and threw them at the soldier then kicked him in his sides. Ursula entered the fight and finding, a big rock, she ran over with it and smashed it onto his face. The soldier's legs kicked and he tried to move, but Kurt and Ludwig relentlessly dug their knives into him. Finally, he was still. Kurt and Ludwig stood up, panting. They stripped him to his underwear, and took anything of value from his dead body. That's when Ludwig felt it.

The holster's buckle had ripped across Ludwig's skin. It startled him. Pushing aside the dead soldier's overcoat, Luddie stared at the pistol with awe. *Should I take it?*

With trepidation, he unsnapped the leather strap that held the gun. The silver shone brightly and his hand trembled as he pulled it out. *Mumma and Poppa would whip my hide if they saw me holding this. But I have to be strong.* He looked over at Ursula, wide-eyed and opened mouthed. "I'll take this for our protection," Ludwig announced to the group.

They all nodded in agreement. He took the clip out and shoved it and the gun into his pocket.

Kurt and Ludwig lugged the dead soldier into a clump of bushes. The other children covered him as well as they could with stones and leafy branches.

"There, that should do it," said Kurt.

Then they walked back to the hut.

Inside the hut, Ludwig slid the gun carefully into his backpack. He turned and saw blood dripping from Ursula's arm. "Urshey, you're hurt! Quick, someone give me a towel!"

Lise brought a towel over to Ludwig and he wiped the blood away. "Good, it's not too deep. We'll just bandage it and you should be fine."

As Ludwig cut the towel into small strips for her arm, the events whirled in Ursula's head.

"Luddie," she started.

"Yes, Urshey?" Ludwig wrapped her arm.

"What was that man going to do to me?" she asked.

He stopped. *What should I tell her?* He grabbed her gently by her shoulders and looked directly into her eyes.

"Were you scared?" he asked.

"Yes, very scared," she nodded.

"That's because he was going to hurt you very, very badly and your common sense knew that. Ursula, always trust your intuition, promise me that."

He finished tying the towel strips around her arm.

"I will," she nodded. "But...you whistled."

His face flushed with redness. *How could I have not seen him?* He backed away from her, shamefully lowered his head, and turned.

Chapter Twelve

Standing up, Ursula pulled the prism necklace from her pocket. She approached Ludwig and held the necklace out to him.

"Here, Luddie. Would you like to look at things in a different way?"

He turned to face Ursula. With reddened eyes and tear-glazed cheeks, he gazed at the crystal prism necklace. He hugged Ursula harder and longer than she ever remembered.

"Thank you, Urshey," he closed her hand around the necklace. "You have to protect the crystal prism. You have to teach the prism principles. Mumma would want that."

She revered her brother with immense adoration. *And you, my brother, are my shining knight.*

Thunder crackled from outside. Ludwig pivoted to face the others.

"We need to leave this hut. The Germans will find his

body, and then they'll be snooping around," Ludwig entreated.

The rain rushed down in a rage.

"We can't leave now, it's pouring outside," stated Nikki.

"We'll leave tomorrow as soon as it is daylight. Is that okay, Luddie?" Kurt asked.

"All right, but as soon as it is daylight," Ludwig agreed adamantly.

The boys sat on their side of the hut, and the girls sat on their side. Kurt whittled a stick while Petr built a teepee with sticks and string. A small fire burned in the concrete hole; Ursula's coat, covering the window, blocked the light. Nikki sat in the corner, pressing her scarf and folding it in different ways. Ursula sat next to Lise on the straw.

"You are lucky to have something of your mother's," Lise remarked to Ursula. Lise remembered how the crystal necklace sparkled when Ursula set it down on the dresser of the first bombed house they'd pillaged. Ursula smiled in acknowledgment.

Then Ursula thought of the others. Lise was right. As Ursula looked around she realized that she was the only one in the group to be in possession of something that belonged to either her mother or father. Yes, she was extremely fortunate. She realized that she couldn't keep the wonderment of the crystal prism principles to herself and so resolved to share the beauty of the prism with the others. She sat straight up and held the necklace out, letting it dangle.

"Look at the wall behind us," she said to Lise.

Lise turned.

"Oh, my," Lise exclaimed. The fire light shone through

the necklace and dozens of small rainbows fluttered on the wall. Lise laughed.

Ursula watched Lise's face beam with joy.

"Wow, that's pretty," Nikki said.

Everyone in the hut watched the rainbows as they danced on the walls and ceiling.

"And see this," Ursula sat down on the straw and summoned Lise. Ursula put one of the crystals up to her eye. "Look through it like this."

She handed it to Lise. Lise put one of the crystals to her eye.

"Wow, beautiful!"

"Turn it from side to side," Ursula instructed.

Lise laughed.

"Mumma said, 'there is more than one way to look at something.'"

"Can I try?" Nikki asked.

Lise handed the necklace to Nikki, who then held it up to her eye.

"Gee, there *is* more than one way to look at something. It's beautiful." She handed the necklace back to Lise. "Thank you, Urshey."

"This is marvelous!" Lise turned to face Ursula. "Thank you so much for sharing it."

Lise looked down at the necklace in her hand. "Urshey, can I sleep with it tonight," she begged with pleading eyes. "I promise I'll give it right back to you in the morning. It's just so pretty, it makes me think of my Mum."

Ursula gulped. *I know I need to share it, but it's all I have left of Mumma's.* "Yes, you can wear it overnight," Ursula granted.

144

"The fire light shone through the necklace and dozens of small rainbows fluttered on the wall."

"Thank you, thank you, thank you!" Lise hugged her. She put the necklace around her neck and lay down on her straw bed. She giggled as she held one of the crystals to her eye and looked through it. Ursula lay down next to her and eventually everyone fell asleep.

In the middle of the night, Lise awoke, sat up and looked around. A tiny flicker of light emanated from the fire. Everyone was still asleep. The rain had stopped.

She had awakened because of a need to relieve her bladder. Though she knew that no one was to go outside alone, *It's a shame to wake them,* Lise thought. *I won't be long, and I won't go far.*

Lise got up quietly and tip-toed out the door. She walked just a few feet away from the hut and urinated. *Ah, that's better now.* She started her way back to the hut, feeling the necklace swaying with her. *I wonder if the moon will shine through the crystal.* As she walked, she held the necklace up high for the moon's rays to shine through. Unknowingly, she stepped onto a pile of wet rocks. In an instant, Lise's feet slipped out from beneath her and she fell onto the rocks. Her head slammed onto a pointy stone and a light flashed before her eyes.

Lise awoke. She didn't know how long she had been sleeping there, but it was still dark. She pushed herself up to a sitting position, tried to stand, but discovered that she had no control over her left leg. Her vision was obscured but, squinting her eyes, she saw the hut in front of her, its door slightly ajar.

I don't know what's wrong with me, she thought. *Why can't I see clearly? Why can't I stand up? But I'm not too far away, maybe I can crawl.*

146

She crept to the hut, drawing her left leg up to her chest with every push. Panting, pulling and dragging, she slowly made her way back to the hut. As soon as she was inside the door, she collapsed.

What's that? Ursula was awakened by something familiar. As in a distant memory, she recognized the shimmer of daylight as it barged into the hut. *But the door is closed, and the coat is in the window,* she recalled. Ursula rolled over and sat up. She saw the others were also waking.

"What? Who opened that door? That door is to be closed at all times," growled Ludwig. They saw Lise lying in front of the door.

"Oh, Lise!" Kurt stood up and went to the door to close it. "Why did you open the door? We don't want any Germans to see us." He closed the door and bent down to wake her. "Lise," he shook her. Her body was stiff. "Uh, oh," Kurt said with a startled look.

"What?" Nikki and Ludwig asked.

Kurt placed his finger on her neck. He couldn't find a pulse.

"Lise's dead," Kurt announced.

"No!" Ursula cried.

They all got up and gathered around Lise.

"Are you sure?" Ludwig asked, stunned.

Kurt nodded, dumbfounded.

"How?"

"Look," Petr said, pointing to her head. A knot of flesh bulged outward from under her scant growth of hair. A splotch of dried blood lay on top and a line of dried blood trickled down the back of her head.

"How did that happen, Luddie?" Ursula asked.

"I don't know," Ludwig answered.

"I don't know either, but she's gone," Kurt remarked.

"Maybe she went outside and fell against something, or maybe someone did this to her," Ludwig stated in a distressed tone. "In any event, it is imperative that we leave immediately!"

"But what are we going to do now? We don't have tools to bury her. We can't just leave her here," Nikki said.

Kurt and Ludwig looked at each other. They knew she was right, but what could they do? The idea came to Ludwig.

"The pit...," Ludwig said to Kurt.

"...With the dead bodies," Kurt agreed.

"You mean you're going to put her in that nasty, big hole with those other dead bodies?" Nikki asked, repugnance etched into her face.

Petr's and Ursula's eyes widened.

"What else can we do?" Kurt and Ludwig asked her.

Nikki's thoughts were stymied. She shook her head in frustration and sat down in the corner. Petr joined her, his arm interlocking hers.

"When do we do it, Luddie?" Kurt asked.

"Certainly not in the daytime, it's too dangerous. We'll have to wait for nightfall. And we'll have to stay in this hut all day," Ludwig said disgustedly. "And let's hope that if this was done by someone that that person is gone."

Ludwig didn't truly believe that the death was at the hands of another person, but he was hoping to scare the others into feeling his sense of urgency of leaving the hut and finishing their journey toward the German border.

Oh, well, it's just one more day.

"Well, we need to move her away from the door for now," Kurt suggested.

"Let's put her in the wheelbarrow and we'll push her outside," Ludwig instructed.

They kept the wheelbarrow inside the hut with them. Kurt and Ludwig lifted her up and carried her to it. They lay her inside and pushed the wheelbarrow just outside the hut's door. Ursula followed them outside carrying Lise's blanket.

"Here, put this over her," Ursula suggested, handing the blanket to Ludwig.

He took the blanket and lay it over her motionless body.

"Luddie, can I have my necklace back?"

"Oh, of course," Luddie replied. He peeled back the blanket to expose her head. Lifting her head gently, he retrieved the necklace from around her neck and handed it to Ursula. "You know, Ursula, because of you, she had a little bit of happiness before she died."

Ursula nodded in agreement then slipped the crystal prism necklace back into her pocket.

Ludwig turned to Kurt and Petr. "We should try to catch a rabbit or two while we're out here because we'll be in the hut all day."

Kurt pulled the string from his pocket and the three of them set out to catch food for the day.

At twilight, as soon as Kurt and Ludwig believed it was safe, they left the hut. Nikki, Petr and Ursula stayed behind. Together, Kurt and Ludwig pushed the wheelbarrow to the mass grave. They dumped Lise with her blanket into the deep hole. Her body thumped.

"Shouldn't we say a prayer or something?" Kurt asked.

"Yeah," Ludwig looked up and said bitterly, "God, get us out of Germany."

They woke the next day and gathered their few belongings into their backpacks and headed out, pushing the wheelbarrow, for the border between Germany and Holland.

"Now, we are going to walk all day, no stopping," Ludwig charged.

Ursula thought he sounded angry.

"The only time we will stop is for dinner and to sleep. Does everyone understand?"

They all nodded their heads.

"Good, let's go." *I will get us out of Germany or die trying,* Ludwig thought. *If only I had been able to bring Lise, too.*

Ludwig, just a teenager, felt the burden of responsibility for her death. He was ashamed and furious with himself. *Aren't I to protect them all?* The punishing thought continued to condemn him.

It was no longer necessary to wear the hats and scarves, for their hair had now grown enough to cover their scalps. Kurt's hair was blond, just as he had said; Nikki's hair was brown and Petr's was black.

Kurt and Ludwig alternated pushing the wheelbarrow. They had decided the quickest way out of Germany was to go straight. They were frightened, but they were just as scared to stay in one place as they were to go forward. So they exited the forest and headed down the decimated road, traveling through war-ravaged fields and bombed towns.

As far as they could see, the debauchery of war was evident. Where there once stood massive buildings, now lay huge piles of rubble. Patches of blue sky twisted among the gray smoke and they could hear gunfire and explosions in the distance as bombers flew overhead.

"We don't look Jewish now," Kurt proposed. "We have regular clothes and hair," he said, patting his head. "Maybe we won't catch the attention of the Germans."

Ludwig wished that were true. In reality he knew that five children walking without parents through a war zone, and pushing a wheelbarrow, would look suspicious. So they kept an eye out for soldiers, and with even the slightest hint of military encroachment, Ludwig commanded everybody to hide.

"If we are near buildings or trees, we will hide behind them," Ludwig instructed. "If nothing is around to conceal us, we will lie flat on the ground, pretending to be dead, until the danger passes."

Ludwig thought of the gun in his backpack and hoped that he would never be forced to use it.

Days went by and, to Ludwig's amazement, most of the German civilians they encountered ignored their tiny group. Ludwig figured that maybe the absurdity of five children fending for themselves was now an unremarkable occurrence.

Hunger and thirst became constant elements. They searched for something, anything, to eat. The scorched land offered little vegetation; even the supply of edible weeds was sorely crippled. Rabbits and other small creatures refused to step outside the safety of the forest, and clean water was just as difficult to find as food.

Some days, as they walked the deteriorated roadways, they would go by small towns with a marketplace.

"Okay, now here's our chance," Kurt said as they huddled together. "Swipe what you can."

They sauntered up to the fruit stand, and inconspicuously grabbed a piece of fruit. They stole as often as they could in every town they traversed. Most of the time they would get caught, and find themselves fleeing from the angry storeowner.

They kept walking. As they passed vacant, bombed houses, they rummaged through them, finding very little. Occasionally, as they passed homes occupied by German citizens, some people would take pity on them and offer them some food and water. The children were grateful, but it was never enough to satisfy, and there never seemed to be enough generous people.

"Luddie," Ursula asked one day, "do you think we'll ever see Poppa and Sophus again?"

He sighed heavily. She was strong, but could she really cope with his answer?

"We'll find them; we'll find every one of our relatives," Kurt interrupted. "I will look for them myself."

Ludwig, unable to give an encouraging word, nodded gratefully at Kurt.

"And Petr and I will go back to Poland," Nikki said.

Petr beamed up at her.

"And we'll find Hilda, too?" Ursula asked.

"Hilda is a traitor. She can go to hell," Ludwig said unremorsefully.

Ursula gasped while Kurt looked at him questioningly.

No, Ludwig would not explain himself to either of them,

nor would he tell what he saw. How vividly his mind recalled her beating the children, and how disgusted he was as he watched the German soldiers fondle her. They walked on.

One day they passed a home and, spying the outside water pump, they decided to fill their jug. Just as the water flowed into their jug, the homeowner angrily stomped out of his house, aiming his shotgun at them. "Get off my property!" he yelled. They ran before he had a chance to fire. The children were more hungry than they had ever been before.

Hunger is an insidious evil, its severity slowly overpowers its victim until the goal of death by starvation is met. At first hunger is just an irritant, a subtle rumbling and a nagging thought of food which can be easily ignored. But if hunger's battle endures, the victim feels lightheaded and irritable while the stomach churns constantly and audibly. Soon the empty stomach cramps in protest and the sufferer feels the urge to vomit, yet there are no contents to expel. The body shakes uncontrollably and the victim feels cold. Soon the victim lapses into emotional, mental and physical apathy. Headaches and dizziness plague the sufferer so that all they care about is food. They cannot concentrate or think clearly and not having the strength to form words correctly, slurring occurs. The stomach alternates between cramping and numbness. Other organ systems begin to slow, eventually breaking down. Strength is diminished, extremities swell, and bodily movements are impaired. The victim falls in and out of consciousness as the heartbeat slows. If nourishment is not given at this point, death will soon triumph.

Hunger's next victims were five children.

They walked for weeks through barren land defiled by bombings. As they lumbered along, their feet dragged along the dirt roads. This, and the sporadic passing civilian vehicle, drizzled their bodies with a fine coat of dust. Ursula's bright blue dress had long since become ragged and discolored, but the flower pocket still clung tightly to the pinafore, encasing the treasure inside.

At night they slept where they could, sometimes in bombed houses, sometimes in a gully alongside the road. Their strength declined rapidly. Kurt and Ludwig refused to push the wheelbarrow any longer and thrust it away. In their frail condition talking became laborious, their heads overtaken by dizziness and headaches. They kept walking. They couldn't remember the last village they had passed or how long they had been without food or water. Ursula trembled and it felt as though her stomach had fallen out of her body, leaving a gaping hole. They trudged along with hunger pangs so severe it weakened their knees, until finally they could no longer stand. Finally, they fell to the ground in an area which looked like it had been a meadow at one time, but now there was nothing but a few leafless trees and brown thistles.

Their heads hurt and their vision was blurred; their dirt-covered bodies jerked uncontrollably. As they lay there, insects and flies lingered across their bodies and faces. They didn't have the strength to bat them away. They couldn't move; all they could do was breathe and think.

We almost made it out of Germany. I guess this is where we'll die, Ludwig thought.

The hot sun beat down on them, inhibiting the ability to breath. They lay there until nightfall.

That night Ursula dreamt of Hanrie, Mumma, Poppa and Sophus. They were home and they were singing and dancing in the front room. Ursula was wearing her tutu. The crystal prism necklace sparkled like a strand of stars around Mumma's neck. Mumma smiled and handed the necklace to Ursula. Then, all at once, the SS burst into the room, shooting Hanrie, Mumma, Poppa and Sophus. They tumbled to the floor in front of her. Ursula looked at the prism necklace in her hand and it was dripping with blood. She gasped, then awoke. It was morning. Ludwig was by her side, and he had heard her stir.

"Urshey," Ludwig managed to mutter. He turned his head. Ursula lay a few feet on his left. She groaned in return. Scattered around him were Kurt, Nikki and Petr. Nikki and Petr lay side by side, moaning.

They lay there the rest of the day, the pain of hunger churning their insides, causing their heads to spin and their bodies to quiver.

We almost made it, Ludwig thought. *I guess this is where we'll die.*

Dusk approached. Then, suddenly, they heard a noise, a loud, flapping noise coming from above. Ludwig looked up and tried to focus on the green dot in the sky. It was a helicopter, but from which army? He squinted his eyes and focused on the flag painted on the side. It was the British! Then he heard Nikki scream.

"No, they're not taking us!"

Ludwig looked over at Nikki. She and Petr were trying

to walk. Her face was twisted with delirium. She and Petr stumbled.

"No, Nikki, it's the Brits!" he yelled to her, but with his weakened voice and her frantic state, she didn't hear him. Ludwig looked in the distance. A military truck with foot soldiers by its side was coming toward them. Nikki was screaming and climbing a tree. Petr followed her.

"Nikki, Petr, stop!" yelled Kurt.

Kurt, Ludwig and Ursula pleaded with Nikki and Petr to stop, but they listened to no one. They continued climbing, clumsily.

They've gone mad, Ludwig thought. The British Army was getting closer. Ludwig could hear the men talking.

"No, they're not getting us!" They heard Nikki yell from atop a branch.

She clung to the branch, crying frantically. Petr scrambled desperately to reach her. Then, suddenly, the dried branch snapped and Nikki, Petr and the branch plummeted to the ground. They hit the ground with a loud thud. Nikki screamed, holding onto her side, but Petr was silent.

"Bring a stretcher, no, make that two!" one of soldiers commanded.

The medics hurried to Nikki and Petr and loaded them onto the stretchers. Nikki writhed and moaned, while Petr remained quiet and still. Ursula watched as the British soldiers carried Nikki and Petr on the stretchers. She looked around and saw the soldiers carrying the feeble bodies of Kurt and Ludwig to the awaiting truck. She amassed the strength to move her hand to her pocket.

With a swell of energy, she pulled the crystal prism necklace from her pocket and put it to her eye. A British soldier was walking toward her. He was smiling, many times over within her prism. He was the most handsome man she had ever seen, and as he leaned down to pick her up, she thought of Hanrie, Mumma, Poppa and Sophus. She wept.

Oh, Mumma, this is finally our good day!

Postscript

The children were transported by truck to a displaced persons camp in Essen, where they were fed and treated for their injuries.

After arriving by plane at a refugee house in Oxbridge, England, Ludwig Swartz was asked to live with a British general who was very impressed with Ludwig's intelligence and ability to speak several languages. He studied foreign languages at a university (name unknown) and after graduating became a UN interpreter. While on assignment in Africa, he contracted and succombed to malaria. Ludwig never married.

Nikki suffered many injuries after her fall from the tree. She was taken by plane to a hospital in Oxbridge, England. She died there three days later.

Petr fell victim to the fall from the tree as well and died in the truck on the way to the displaced persons camp.

Kurt, now an adult, was determined to go home to Czechoslovakia. Not wanting to be transported to England, he awoke one night and ran away from the displaced persons camp. He was never heard from again.

Frederick Swartz contracted typhus in Bergen-Belsen and died.

Hilda Swartz survived the concentration camp. When the camp was liberated by the British in 1945, Hilda went back to Glashütte. Though she had become pregnant in the camp, her baby was not born until after liberation. When last heard of, she and her daughter had moved to Australia. Hilda has relinquished all contact with her family.

No record has ever been found of Sophus Swartz. No one has seen her or heard of her since the Nazis took her away from her siblings in Bergen-Belsen.

Ursula Swartz was taken by plane to a refugee house, an old mansion in Oxbridge, England. She remained there for two and a half years before a relative, a maternal aunt, was located. Now, approximately ten years old, the aunt took her to London, where they lived with a wounded veteran the aunt attended to.

Ursula and her aunt did not get along. Instead of Ursula going to school, she was forced to perform domestic menial labor. Then, one day, Ursula could not move her muscles. She was taken to a local hospital and diagnosed with rheumatoid arthritis. While in the hospital another maternal aunt was located. Ursula subsequently went to live with that aunt after her discharge from the hospital.

As a young adult, Ursula hiked across Europe. It was during her travels through Italy that she met an American named Milton Block. Milton was an officer in the Maritime Merchant Marines. He just happened to be in the Italian port giving tours of ships when Ursula requested a tour. He was immediately smitten. She came to the United States at his request and married him. Ursula and Milton had three children.

Milton was diagnosed with leukemia and died at the age of sixty-two. Ursula currently lives in Maryland . She still has the necklace.

For more information about Bergen-Belsen...

BOOKS

Hanna Levy-Hass and Anna Hass, *Diary of Bergen-Belsen: 1944-1945*. Chicago, IL: Haymarket Books, 2009.

Abel S. Herzberg and Jack Santcross, *Between Two Streams: A Diary from Bergen-Belsen*. London: Tauris Parke Paperbacks, 2008.

Hadassah Rosensaft, *Yesterday: My Story*. Washington, DC: Holocaust Survivors' Memoirs Project, 2004.

Ben Shephard, *After Daybreak: The Liberation of Bergen-Belsen, 1945*. New York: Schocken Books, 2005.

Luba Tryszunska-Frederick, Ann Marshall, and Michelle Roehm McCann. *Luba: The Angel of Bergen-Belsen*. New York: Tricycle Press, 2003.

MUSEUMS

Bergen-Belsen Memorial Museum (Gedenkstätte Bergen-Belsen)
29303 Lohheide, Germany
(49) (0)5 051 47 59 10
www.bergenbelsen.de

El Paso Holocaust Museum and Study Center
715 N. Oregon
El Paso, TX 79902
(915) 351-0048
www.elpasoholocaustmuseum.org

Florida Holocaust Museum
55 5th St., South
St. Petersburg, FL 33701
(727) 820-0100
www.flholocaustmuseum.org

Holocaust Center of Northern California
121 Steuart St.
San Francisco, CA 94105
(415) 777-9060
www.hcnc.org/contact.html

Holocaust Education and
Resource Center of
Rhode Island
401 Elmgrove Ave.
Providence, RI 02906
(401) 453-7860
www.hercri.org/

Holocaust Memorial
1933-1945 Meridian Ave.
Miami Beach, FL 33139
(305) 538-1663
www.holocaustmmb.org/

Holocaust Memorial and
Tolerance Center of Nassau
County/Welwyn Preserve
100 Crescent Beach Rd.
Glen Cove, NY 11542
(516) 571-8040
www.holocaust-nassau.org

Holocaust Memorial Center
Zekelman Family Campus
28123 Orchard Lake Rd.
Farmington Hills, MI 48334
(248) 553-2400
www.holocaustcenter.org

Holocaust Memorial
Foundation of Illinois
4255 Main St.
Skokie, IL 60076
(847) 677-4640
www.hmfi.org

Holocaust Museum &
Studies Center of the Bronx

High School of Science
75 W. 205th Street
Bronx, NY 10468
(718) 367-5252
www.bxscience.edu/
holocaust/Holocaust.htm

Holocaust Museum and
Learning Center/St. Louis
12 Millstone Campus Dr.
St. Louis, MO 63146
(314) 432-0020
www.hmlc.org/

Holocaust Museum Houston
5401 Caroline St.
Houston, TX 77004
(713) 942-8000
www.hmh.org/
au_history.shtml

Los Angeles Museum of the
Holocaust/Martyrs'
Memorial
6435 Wilshire Blvd., Suite
303
Los Angeles, CA 90048
(323) 651-3704
www.lamoth.org/

Museum of Jewish Heritage-
A Living Memorial
to the Holocaust
Edmond J. Safra Plaza, 36
Battery Place
New York, NY 10280
(646) 437-4200
www.mjhnyc.org/

New Mexico Holocaust and
Intolerance Museum
616 Central Ave. SW
Albuquerque, NM 87102
(505) 247-0606
www.nmholocaustmuseum.org/

Safe Haven Museum &
Education Center
2 East 7th Street
Oswego, NY 13126-1197
(315) 342-3003
www.oswegohaven.org/

Simon Wiesenthal Center
1399 South Roxbury Drive
Los Angeles, CA 90035
(310) 553-8403
www.museumoftolerance.com

Simon Wiesenthal Center-
Museum of Tolerance
226 East 42nd St.
New York, NY 10017
(212) 697-1180
www.wiesenthal.com

Southwest Florida
Holocaust Museum
4760 Tamiami Trail
Naples, FL 34109
(239) 325-4444
www.hmswfl.org/

United States Holocaust
Memorial Museum
100 Raoul Wallenberg Pl , SW
Washington, DC 20024-2126

(202) 488-0400
www.ushmm.org/

Virginia Holocaust Museum
2000 East Cary St.
Richmond, VA 23223
(804) 257-5400
www.va-holocaust.com/

About the Author

"Growing up and living with a Holocaust survivor is a humbling experience. I had the desire to write my mother's story when I was in my early twenties, but she was not receptive at that time. Then one day, decades later, she was talking to a man who told her that he didn't think the Holocaust ever happened. She was angered, and she cried, and now out of that saddening confrontation, an incredible story has emerged."

The author lives in Pennsylvania and is employed at a local area hospital as a Medical Lab Technician.

Other titles from

Gihon River Press, Inc.

BITTER FREEDOM
By Jafa Wallach

Bitter Freedom

Memoir of a Holocaust Survivor   Jafa Wallach

"In spite of the many endless hours spent reading personal narratives and memoirs about the tragedy of the Holocaust, no rendition has engaged me to the extent of utter and complete rage toward man's inhumanity toward man. then Jafa Wallach's *Bitter Freedom* did so quite effortlessly. Ms. Wallach is due praise and awe for this raw truth about the unspeakable atrocities suffered by her family and countless other innocent Jews. I highly recommend this book."

—Janis F. Kearney, personal diarist to President William J. Clinton,
    Author, *Cotton Field of Dreams: A Memoir*

ISBN: 978-0-9819906-3-7 $18.95

SILENCE NOT, A Love Story
By Cynthia L. Cooper

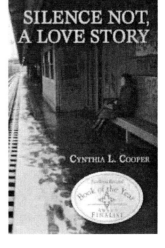

SILENCE NOT, A LOVE STORY

CYNTHIA L. COOPER

Cynthia Cooper is a powerful playwright. *Silence Not, A Love Story* will spark a fabulous discussion on resistance today. Gisa and Paul have incredible moral courage and a life-long-love that sustains them through a terrible period in history when society failed. Each of us needs to consider our character at every moment—are we perpetrator, victim, helper, bystander, or resister? Every high school student should read this play.

—Maureen McNeil, Director of Education,
    The Anne Frank Center USA

ISBN: 978-0-9819906-0-6 $17.95

Available at your favorite book store or library and through Baker & Taylor, Follett and Unique Books and in Australia, John Reed Book Distribution. Available as an ebook from Kindle or Smashwords.com

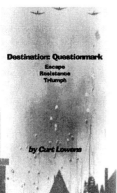

Destination: Questionmark
By Curt Lowens
Coming in January 2013

Visit us on the web at www.gihonriverpress.com
To contact the publisher go to gihonriverpress@msn.com
or call 917.612.8857